STAR-CROSSED

Enakshi J.

Published by InkQuills Publishing House
www.inkquills.in

First Edition 2020

ISBN: 978-81-946962-4-7

For me.

Contents

I
AVYAN

1

A New Lease of Life

January 2017

The balmy rays woke me from the slumber and I could not help but grab the pillow from the other side of the bed and place it on my face. Yes, it blocked the light but the bothersome noise of the drilling machine propelled me to get up. It was Sunday. Who works on a Sunday? The joy of being in a new place, or rather a new country, overrode my tantrum. Yes, I was in New York, the hive of activity. Oh, how desperately I had waited for this moment! I drew the mustard coloured curtains and tried to soak in the winter sun. The intricate floral design on the curtain caught my attention. I had seen something of that sort before. I spent five minutes walking down the memory lane but the beep of my phone interrupted the intensity of my musings. It's time. It was time to explore the area and figure out certain things.

At nine, I stepped out of my 650 sq. feet rented studio apartment and realized that New York was a walking city. I saw a fewer number of cars and that broke my heart. There were people everywhere- kids running on the pavement in fancy costumes, elderly walking with a newspaper, youngsters out on a walk with their dogs and couples sitting on the grey iron benches. There were jubilation, elation and delight in the atmosphere. It felt good. Living this life had been my dream and there I was, just a few hours away from my first day at The New York Times. To accept the role of an Advertising Manager was a bone of contention as my parents did not approve at first. But with constant badgering and persuasion, they gave in.

Unmarried at 30, I did not intend on tying a knot anytime soon. I did not believe in the concept of marriages. The thought of living with someone else, bearing children and metamorphosing into a responsible adult made my heart skip a beat. I was happy being an eccentric male who was a total control freak. I loved working. I loved travelling too. A middle-aged man, who faltered and stopped in the mid-stride, thereby spilling his hot latte all over my light blue t-shirt, yet again disturbed my introspective moment. I didn't know how to react. Had I been in India, I would have shouted, abused, and got into a squabble. Nevertheless, here things were different. I didn't want to be in the limelight and that was the reason I smiled gently and said 'It's okay'. That was contrary to my outlandish self. I brushed aside that thought and headed towards the trailer selling hot dogs. Hungry and excited, I bought something to eat and sat on one of those same grey benches alone and observed the skyscrapers with the tinted glass of blue, green and brown. I loved it. I loved my life.

It was 12:00 PM and I was still at Times Square 42 Street- just a few blocks away from where my office was. I relished the thought that I lived close-by but at the same time, I wondered if I would be able to cope with everything. Anti-social and an introvert by nature, I have a hard time when it comes to making friends. Leaving the worrying part for the next few days, I decided to pamper myself a little more by going shopping. After all, the first impression is definitely the last impression, isn't it?

At 5 in the evening, I returned to my apartment only to find that I had forgotten the keys in an Original Penguin Store. In my frenzy, I banged the door of my neighbour. Within seconds, the black door opened with a click and literally, a tall, dark and handsome man greeted me with a dubious expression. I had a sudden feeling that we would become the best friends. His Adam's apple vividly evident, I noticed his wrist cords bulging like roots of an oak. With teased platinum hair, he looked suave. As soon as he said 'Hi', I noticed his neck muscles become drumhead tight. I acknowledged the greeting and turned my face the other side in a futile attempt to hide my antipathy. I visualized my cheeks being covered in the green of envy. Suddenly, I felt an assuaging touch on my shoulder.

'Hi there, dude!'

Caught unawares, I put forward my hand. We introduced each other and I got to know that he was Mike from the Red Lobster. I pretended to know what that name meant but he seemed to be good at the guesswork.

'It's a restaurant down the road.'

'So, you work there?' I asked projecting my idiocy. I was horrible at making conversations. I knew that and there, I did that again.

'Obviously. I am the manager.'

In an attempt to conceal my embarrassing moment, I asked, 'Can you keep my bags with you so that I can go to the store I forgot my keys at?'

'Which store is it?'

'Original Penguin. Probably at the billing counter. I'll be quick. Please just keep my bags with you for a while.'

'Dude, I have a friend who works there. Wait, let me give him a call and check.'

As his fingers moved on the phone's screen, I noticed a lighter patch of skin on the third finger. Was he suffering from Vitiligo? Poor fellow! I started praying for him and asked God to bless him with a healthy life.

'Robby will come in another five minutes and give your keys.'

'No, no, I can walk and get them,' I asserted.

'He has a bike; he can bring them faster.' I thanked him and waited for the next response like a baffled idiot.

'Why don't you come inside for a bit?'

Should I bother him further? Should I refuse politely? I had to answer; the pause seemed awkward. I managed a slight nod and entered his small apartment. Not that my apartment was bigger than Mike's, but he had more stuff and therefore, less space.

We spent time talking about life in New York. Mike seemed like a nice person. He had his share of woes and weal. However, he was a happy man. He was also unmarried and I thought I would share an affable bond with him.

Alas! It was ten in the night and I was back in my room. I felt accomplished. I had shopped, I had eaten and I had made a friend that day or so I thought. I opened the packet and tried on the suit once more thereby allowing my mind to travel to a cloud-cuckoo-land where I was the centre of the attraction! I looked good. But I knew that was a half-baked truth.

I microwaved the pork bun that I had bought from a food trailer. It looked sumptuous. The sound of my phone alerted me again and I rushed to check the message. It was from the office. I had to report at seven. No delay. Switching on the TV, I spread my blanket on the bed and put my heavy head on the feathery pillows. It felt good. But I wondered for how long!

2

Quelle Surprise

It was early morning; I woke up to the sound of my alarm clock. It had already been four days in New York and I still felt that I had not adjusted to the surroundings. Every day I reached late to work. Those scary big eyes of my boss made me jump out of my skin. I had started sleeping early but to no avail. As the whistle of the old vintage kettle that I had purchased from a garage sale nearby blew, I sprinted to the bathroom to take a hot shower. It was January and the deserted streets increased the cinematic tension of the scene. The birds weren't chirping, the horns weren't blowing - only the faint aroma of hot chocolate hovered in the air. Just then, Skype made a sound and I knew (from the timing) that it was my mother. Like every other Indian mother, she was not only worried about my breakfast but also about me being wooed by the foreign beauties. She believed that one day, I would return to my homeland with a foreign wife more by accident than by design. I didn't find any logic in her beliefs; I didn't have the energy to argue the toss either.

Another hour passed and the hands of the clock stood in a straight line. I grabbed the toast and gulped it down with hot chocolate. My phone rang.

'Where are you?' Bobby asked.

'On the way. Will be there in ten,' I replied.

Bobby was my co-partner in the company; well, actually, he was younger than me but I considered him my sidekick. He knew his way around NYT and that was a blessing in disguise for me. As I pedalled my way through the streets of New York, I glanced at the shops on the way. I tried to play a random guess game in my mind. I passed through the W

42nd street and it was mostly crowded. But mornings were still better. That area was always bustling with noise. With Madame Tussauds just around the corner and McDonalds a few blocks away, that place offered everything- right from eating joints to entertainment. Even the very famous Empire State Building was nearby. Bobby had told me. He had promised to take me along one day.

I met Bobby on my second day at work. He had been on medical leave for quite some time. Since his cabin was right next to mine, I went to him to ask about the photocopy room. And that was how we first interacted. He is jovial and intelligent. He said he wanted to work with The Wall Street Journal because it houses some of the most talented marketing professionals. This job in NYT would give a boost to his career or so he believed. He is 28- quite young and in love with Sam. He is my pillar of strength here.

I reached the main gate of my building and scurried to park my bicycle. The sparkle of the glass annoyed me but it soon vanished as I made my way inside the building.

My office was on the seventh floor and as I waited outside the elevator, I felt an uncompassionate tap on my shoulder.

'Quelle Surprise,' I croaked.

'Do you speak Spanish?' queried Peter.

'More of your conversation would infect my brain,' I wanted to say but all that escaped my generous mouth was 'It's French'.

'Showing off, aren't you?' he smirked.

'No,' I fumbled to find the right words, 'just a habit I developed after listening to Enter Shikari's Quelle Surprise on repeat.'

The information bollixed him; I gave myself an imaginary self-high-five for the miniscule victory.

'Is the proposal for the Verismo Communications ready?' he asked.

'Arr…what?'

'The proposal I asked you to draft yesterday?'

'No, you didn't ask me to do anything of such kind.'

'Ridiculous! How dare you give excuses for not doing the assigned work?'

Baffled and agitated at the same time, I decided to keep the reigns of my tongue under control. As we reached the seventh floor and the door opened, I saw Bobby waiting by the side.

'Bobby, this nitwit has not yet drafted the proposal. Get it done. Soon.' Peter demanded and stormed off.

'I have no idea when he told me to do it,' I tried to explain.

Reading the pain in my voice, Bobby gestured with his hand and asked me to follow him into his cabin. He started rummaging through a large stack of papers- filed and unfiled, both. Holding a light blue file up in the air, he said triumphantly, 'Here, this will save you. He told you to draft a proposal when he said the other day- *Verismo Communications* is growing in business.'

'What do you mean?'

'Peter's brain is as fat as butter and with his foolish gestures he can drive anyone mad. When we were discussing the benefits of having Tanny Cole on our team, he told you that *Verismo Communications* is growing in business. That was enough for me to understand that he was expecting you to be ready with a proposal today. I have done it for you already. Go throw it at his toad-face.'

'Dude, I owe you this one,' I resounded.

The rest of the day was placid. Peter kept looking at me through his glass wall as I crossed his chamber a few times. The surprised look on his face gave me a joy to behold. His ferret-like eyes tried to trace every movement of mine.

At noon, Bobby and I meandered on New York streets to find something good to eat. We ended up in Capizzi and ordered a large *Pepperoni, Portobello Mushrooms & Onions with Iced Tea*. Bobby is a food lover. I, on the contrary, don't have any specific preferences. In four days, I had already eaten in three new restaurants- all thanks to Bobby. Back at Pittsburgh, where his house is, he has a younger sister, Jade, who is seventeen and doing a course on Communications from the University of Pittsburgh. He says she is rational and brainy. Even he is but his long blonde hair speaks of him otherwise.

As we scurried into our cabins after a heavy lunch, our lethargic brains failed to co-operate. And to our horror, Peter entered as a fait accompli. Rubbing the freckles across his nose with his sausage fingers, he pointed at my watch.

'Do you want it, sir?' I rebuked my stupidity immediately.

He fumed in anger and yelled, 'Is this the time to come back from lunch?'

Before I could think of any lame excuse and cover up my folly, Bobby intervened, 'Guess whom we met near the Bowling Lounge- Tanny Cole and she seemed quite amused with the idea of working with us.'

'That woman with a February face won't get everything at her beck and call. Call everyone for an urgent meeting in the conference room in half-an–hour. And you, Avyan- how could you think that I would ask for your flimsy watch? I wanted you to check the time, if that's what your watch is capable of doing.'

I watched Peter's back as he scampered to his cabin. Bobby gave me an empathetic look.

'He hates me,' I admitted.

'He hates everyone,' Bobby consoled.

I wondered when I would be able to comprehend Peter's unreasonable comments. But soon I lost the track of the muddied desire and focused on the meeting that was being called to convince the board for not hiring Tanny Cole.

'Why would you bring up Tanny in the conversation?' I elbowed Bobby as we sat at the large conference table.

'Two reasons- one, only her name could have saved us in that situation, and two, Peter hates that woman. He does exactly the opposite of what he is told, and thus, I played the masterstroke. Haven't you heard of Reverse Psychology?'

I applauded Bobby's wit and spontaneity in my mind and patted his back.

After ending the game of hiring new candidates on check and mate, we headed to Capizzi again to binge on another round of round bread loaded with cheese. Just when we asked the attender to bring the bill, we saw a man raising a toast, actually a coke, to his wife. All the people around us started cheering and we joined the gang. But soon our excitement faded away as we spotted Peter sitting beside the woman in the limelight. It took us nanoseconds to realize that the woman was Peter's wife. With my eyes on stalks, I turned my head towards Bobby and realized that he already had his eyebrows raised.

Peter's wife was wearing a glamorous green dress- some different kind of green. I wondered how she tolerated Peter at home.

'To my darling, to my beloved- the one who makes me complete…' cheered Peter but was cut off midway by his wife.

'Oh, cut to the chase, Peter. You are sounding cheesy.'

And surprisingly, he shut up. That was the flipside of his personality and we didn't know about it. How can he behave differently with us? With my mind flooded with numerous such questions, I gestured Bobby to tiptoe our way out of the restaurant before Peter found the bait to prey on.

As we reached closer to Times Square, we heaved a sigh of relief. Bobby put his hand on my shoulder and stared at me. Within seconds I understood what he meant and we burst out laughing. 'Quelle Surprise,' I said.

He nodded and we headed to our homes.

Just outside my building, on the rough footpath, as I walked towards the gate of my building, I heard faint whimpering. I turned around to locate the source but was unable to see any person. I started walking again and unexpectedly, a dog clung to my leg. She whimpered. I noticed that she was quite frail. When I touched her fur, she licked my face. At that moment, I realized that I would no longer be alone in my 650 sq. ft. apartment.

3

Pleased as Punch

Lying on a white, sandy beach, I could feel the sun beating down on my bronzed body. With brisk footsteps, a gorgeous Canadian boy headed towards me and attempted to refill my empty Silver Monk glass. The crystal-clear ocean water invited me with its open arms. I wiped off the sand from my face and lay on my back soaking the tepid light. Just when I was ready to enter my day dreaming mode, Bobby splashed a bucketful of sand on my face. I screamed in horror as the sand seeped into my eyes. He apologized instantly and started explaining how his bothersome girlfriend had caused unrest in his otherwise boring life. I played along and told him how lucky he was to have her; she tried to bring some joy in his life. Red with anger, he punched my stomach.

'Hey man, what is your problem? I was just kidding,' I said with utmost annoyance. Suddenly I developed a sinking feeling; the fruit salad that I had gulped in seemed to fizzle in my fist-sized stomach. I opened my mouth to puke but nothing came out. The fluttering in my gut continued.

'Avy, you always make fun of my relationship. I don't know how to explain it to you. Sam has become the bane of my life. She spends so much on her clothes that I am left with nothing by the end of the month.'

I guffawed and saw the lines on Bobby's forehead shrinking into a frown. He didn't like it when I did that. And I enjoyed doing it even more. His phone beeped and I saw a photo popping up on his screen. Like a flash, he pushed the phone towards me and gestured. I understood but I pretended. He insisted.

'Hey Sam,' I smirked, 'how are you?'

'Hi Avyan. Can you please give the phone to Bobby?'

'Uhhh, well, actually, he just went to get a drink. You can leave a message for him,' I said trying to sound as convincing as possible.

'Well, in that case, please remind him to upgrade his card. There is hardly any money left and I have to buy him a nice birthday gift.'

'Then why don't you use your card,' I responded and waited like a cat on hot bricks. She was offended. Yes, she was. I should not have said so. I stole a glance at Bobby and there it was. His sullen expression made me break out in a cold sweat. I knew I had made things worse for him.

'Sorry,' I whispered, trying to apologize to the angry young man before me and to the phony Latin American on the other side of the phone.

A few hours later, when the sun's rays were slant and the light was dimmer, I stood up to gather my things. I introspected. My life was amazing. Yes, it had taken a while to convince Bobby to spend that Sunday on the beach but he had eventually agreed. Brighton Beach was one of the most famous beaches in New York. I always wanted to go there with my friends. Though Bobby wanted to bring along Samantha, better known as Sam, she opted for shopping instead.

Both of them had been together for three months. They had met at a local pub, Frying Pan, where Bobby and I had gone to get away from the busy city life. While I quenched my stress with a drink, Bobby's fatigue was doused by Sam, who worked in that bar.

I opened the zipper of my duffle bag and placed my things inside neatly. Complacent and happy with the arrangement,

I signalled Bobby to start walking. The weather was changing. I thought that it might rain. The bright blue of the sky was transformed into a plain surface with plenty of purple bruises. A light wind carried a film of sand hissing up against our legs. Klutzy and clumsy that Bobby was, he tripped and fell on his face. I chuckled and immediately hid the laughter behind a partly genuine concern.

'Are you ok?'

'I think I am.'

'How did you fall?'

'Something caught hold of my thumb and pulled me deeper into the sand.'

'What?'

Curbing my desire to convulse, I tried to get his foot out of the small sandpit created by his body weight. He was right. Something had caught hold of his thumb and that something was a keyring. I forgot about the pain of my dear friend and focused on the keyring. It was pretty. With some letters embossed on its surface, it made a tinkling sound. I shook it in an attempt to brush off the sand. It read- A… (heart) NEWYORK. Probably someone with a name that began with 'A' must have left it there. I stretched my arm to throw the keyring but the sudden urge of keeping it with me overrode the first thought. It was nice and my name began with 'A' too. Why not keep it? I could use it. I squandered 5 minutes into contemplating whether to keep that keyring or not. In spite of noticing a bronze key hanging from the metal ring, I deliberately ignored it.

'Dude, come on, it's getting dark.' Bobby chimed in. The slight wind was enough to make his long hair sway and caress his eyes repeatedly. He ran his hands through his golden-brown hair and forced me to admit (in my mind) that he was handsome. I slid the keyring into my pocket and started making plans about using it for office purposes.

A day at Brighton Beach was what everyone looked forward to. Sadly, I had to go to work the next day and sign many proposals. The NYT was coming up with a new quarterly print magazine and they were planning to call it 'NY Cult'. I had to discuss the budget with the sponsors and give a defined layout of the marketing plan. It was a tough job, but I liked it here. If given a chance to settle here permanently, I would jump the bandwagon instantly without giving it a second thought.

As the morning sun peeped into my bedroom, my new pet, Scarlet, jumped on my chest leaving me gasping for breath. I had found her eating leftovers on the pavement. Feeling sympathetic, I had brought this devil home a few days back. Furry and playful, Scarlet, was a husky who was possibly abandoned by her owner. She was extremely crabby; she jumped all day long but when she lay by my side at night, she gave out a blood-curdling growl. I thought she dreamt her doggy dreams and chased either an imaginary rabbit or a mouse in those dreams. Her fur and her smell kickstarted my day.

At 6, I applied butter on the toast and poured myself a cup of hot milk. I decided to wear formals that day because two presentations were lined up. Giving final touches to my suit and my gelled hair, I scurried out of my apartment and ran into Mike.

'Hey dude, what's up?'

'Hey Mike. I shall catch up with you in the evening. Running late already,' I jabbered and without waiting for his response, I darted out of the door guarding the staircase. Tripping suddenly and then regaining my balance, I thanked my stars for saving me.

New York was a lively city. Early in the morning, you could spot several early risers out for the walk. Health was vital for people there. Unlike in my country, I did not see people spending their time and energy on the idiot box lest they become idiot themselves! I unlocked the bicycle and braced myself for a hasty ride.

At 6:50, I entered the big blue glass door, swiped my ID card and greeted the guard with a cordial smile. I was bang on time and I praised myself for that. As I waited for the lift to come, I looked through the pages inside my brown folder. Nothing seemed legible. Blame my blurry vision or the mental turbulence, I was not able to read the points. I still made a desperate yet futile effort. Before I could say Jack Robinson, I felt a strong push and flung all my papers in the air. Tears hung by fingernails on the edges of my eyelids. It was rightly said never trouble trouble until trouble troubles you! I turned my head around to see who the culprit was but ended up with a mild sprain in the neck.

'Aah!' I mumbled, 'I guess it is my unlucky day today.'

'Excuse me!' she avowed rather forcefully.

Before I could even know who asked me to excuse her rather than saying 'sorry', I saw the door of the elevator close. All I knew was that the callous female was wearing a beige overcoat and her hair were tied with the help of a golden clip. I hexed my fate and bent to pick my papers. The rest of the day was kosher.

At six, I wound up my work and scampered out of the office; I didn't want to keep Bobby waiting. We had planned to visit the Empire State Building because it was close to our place and luckily, he got free early that day. Maybe it was just me who had had a bad day, after all!

Hours later, Bobby and I were sitting at the table at Keens Steakhouse, contemplating our life decisions and waiting for the beer to take the reins of our intelligent mind in its hands. In another hour or so, I passed out. The next thing I knew was that it was Tuesday (the next day) and I was lying on my bourgeois bed with my shoes on. Hallucinating with absurd dreams, I jumped out of the bed and splashed cold water on my face. The cell phone gallery was flooded with imprudent photographs of Bobby. Appalled, I could not take my eyes off the fifth picture that had me showing my bum to the crowd. 'How can I do all of this?' I banged my head on the wall as I asked myself this rhetorical question!

Bobby, too, must have seen something weird about last night's photos as he had called me repeatedly. I pretended that nothing had happened but eventually gave in. It had been sixteen days already and I didn't miss home at all. I liked it here even after I had made a fool of myself in front of the strangers. Maybe this new euphoric energy was missing in my life when I was back at home. This energy propelled me to work hard during the day and then let my hair down in the evening. Bobby had become a good friend. He was still under the impression that Sam loved him and was planning to tell his family soon about her. I still had no plans for marriage. It was not my cup of tea.

I spent the rest of the day at home studying for the presentations that had been rescheduled for next Monday. To ease the stress on my eyes, I shut them for a moment. Startled by the unexpected vision, I opened them. The woman in the beige coat flashed in my mind. Just like how they project the mosaiced faces on television, I could not see her face. I could not recall her basic body structure. I only remembered the coat. That demonic coat!

I brushed aside all the thoughts and called it a night. I picked up the soiled plates that reeked of boiled veggies and boiled eggs, put them in the sink and decided to wash them in the morning. Just then, Scarlet came running towards me and imitated some of my speaking words. I instantly knew what she wanted. I tossed a piece of bacon at her which was kept ready. She wagged her tail and acknowledged. I waited for her to finish and then we headed to bed.

4

A Close Shave

As the loops of white smoke surrounded me, I started questioning my sanity. It was Bobby's idea to talk to Brenda. He wanted to set me up with her. And I hated the idea. We came up to the 13th floor where Brenda worked (I think as a newsletter head or something), only to find her missing from her desk. When we asked a couple of her neighbours, we came to know that she was out for a smoke. And there we were standing inside the smoking room, waiting for Brenda to finish her chore.

'Hey Bob, how have you been?' questioned Brenda patting Bobby hard on his back.

'I have been great. For some reason, I was feeling a little off today. But when you came along, you changed my mood,' finished Bobby with a coquettish grin.

Brenda glanced at me and said, 'Have I changed your mood too?'

'No, it is pretty much the same,' I said boorishly.

'Who is this new friend of yours?'

'He is Avyan- Avy- or better Avyan, the new advertising manager. He is very intelligent.' Bobby conceded.

'That's very jocular,' I snapped at him.

Brenda didn't seem to like my tartness. She excused herself gesturing at her phone and I got the hint. I grabbed Bobby by his elbow and pulled him into a corner.

'What was that?'

'Is your ass jealous of the amount of shit that just came out of your mouth?' ranted Bobby.

'Are you always this stupid or are you making a special effort today?'

'Dude, why would you speak like that to Brenda?'

'Because I am not interested in getting a date for myself. Is it so difficult to understand?'

'If you continue pouring mud on my efforts, you will die single.'

I flashed a smile and gestured him to get back to work.

At 01:00 PM, I got up from my chair to stretch my legs and get some fresh air. I was working on a new proposal for Poilter Agency. Tracing back their presence in the market, I realized that they were a blue-chip company and landing them in NYT's kitty would not only impress Peter but also increase my chances of getting promoted the next year. That was how they rolled there. Land the biggest fish in the net and you will become the boss' right hand. Or that's what Bobby had told me the day before. I sauntered around and glanced at other people's work. Some of them greeted me while others hushed me off. The moment I saw Peter walking towards my cabin, I hopped, skipped and jumped back to my seat.

'I see you are free,' he grimaced.

'Not really. I am working on some pending files. Do you want anything?'

Instantly, I realized that I had asked a wrong question. Cursing my folly, I waited for the unwanted.

'No. I just came to inform that I'll be on leave for two days- have a wedding to attend in Brooklyn.'

God bless this man. How wonderful the workplace will become when he is not around. I can also finish my proposal and give him a surprise when he comes back. I thought. Like a happy camper, I dialled extension number 8 and gurgled, 'The boss will be on leave for two days. Want to grab a beer to celebrate?'

'Yes' came the reply from the other side. It wouldn't take anyone more than a second to guess that the person on the other side was Bobby, of course.

The next day I woke up like the prince of the city, made myself a cup of hot coffee, fed Scarlet and got dressed in casuals. It was a good day to let the formals stay at home. On my way to the office, I bought that day's newspaper and a cheese and ham sandwich. It gave me immense pleasure when I read The New York Times, for I felt proud. There was so much more to this country than we already knew. Take for instance, that sandwich- Plump ham, sautéed with chile flakes and served with a salad of oyster mushrooms, onions, corn and cucumber and the soft cheese that oozed out of this homespun masterpiece- that was all I wanted on a Tuesday morning- fresh, sumptuous and creamy!

I parked my bicycle and stood by the bench on the footpath to finish my breakfast. Just then, a fierce gold sparkle nearly made me blind. I squinted and tried to peer through the narrow gaps between my fingers- it was Brenda. Putting my hand half-up in the air to wave at her, I whispered 'Hi' and barely survived the most humiliating moment of my life. Brenda looked at me, ignored and walked away. Glad that

Bobby was nowhere around to enjoy the scene; I brought my hand down and rushed inside the NYT building.

'Hey dude, look at you! All shiny and happy?' smirked Bobby.

'Obviously.' And we broke into a hysterical laugh.

'So, how's your big fish progress?'

'Going on. I have found a potential client,' I said joyfully.

'Good, I won't ask you anything more lest anyone else hears it. See you at lunch.'

I turned my chair back towards the desk and opened the file to type. But that day was just not the day to work. How frequently did anyone get a chance to waste time when Peter was away and hadn't assigned any work? I minimized the screen and pulled out the newspaper from my messenger bag. But before that I got myself a hot cup of coffee. I didn't like the coffee there; it's the machine coffee. I liked the traditionally brewed one- café Americano. What I read next on the front page, left me rooted to the spot- 'This is Poilter Agency, the most dangerous US company you've never heard of'. Ignoring my coffee, I diverted my full attention to that article.

Poilter Agency is the largest broadcast company in America. But its bigoted politics – and connections to the White House – are raising concerns. Most Americans don't know it exists. Primetime US news refers to it as an "under-the-radar company". Unlike Mint News and Fredrick Muttin, virtually no one outside of business circles could name its CEO. And yet, Poilter Agency is the owner of the largest number of TV stations in America.

"Poilter Agency is probably the most dangerous company most people have never heard of," said Trevor Mann, the chairman of Federal Communications Commission (FCC), the top US broadcast regulator.

"Maybe the most influential media company you never heard of"- another was recorded saying.

I looked for the writer's name but to my utter dismay, I only saw 'Senior Editor- NYT' as the signature. A sudden dread hit my core. What once seemed like the only chance I had to rise and shine now seemed like the well filled with slush and grease. Whosoever was the Senior Editor at NYT had saved my day by writing about Poilter Agency. A shaky and slow smile built up as the surprise or rather the shock sank in. I dialled Bobby's number.

'Hey, come to the cafeteria as soon as possible. I have to tell you something really important.'

'What is it?' he enquired.

'Wait till you meet me in person,' I slurred.

'Please, a slight hint at least?' he begged.

'Be there in ten minutes.' I put the receiver down, drank my coffee that had taken in the cold air and changed its temperature and logged off my computer screen.

As I moved towards the main reception area, I saw two men looking impatiently at the receptionist. When I moved a little closer, I realized they were from Poilter Agency and had come to our office to subpoena on the grounds of public defamation. They kept saying that they wanted to meet Adah Sharma. I wondered who that person was. The name sounded fascinating but at the same time, the urge to understand the big picture kept me on my feet. I pressed the button on the side of the elevator (which had sunken into its socket because of the everyday pressure) and waited for the elevator to come.

'Excuse me,' a familiar voice rebuked me. It took me a few milliseconds to recall the face; it was the lady in the beige overcoat. As she scorned at me, I recalled my mistake. Everything about Poilter Agency had been so overwhelming that I was in a dream world of my own. I had collided with her just a few moments back when I made a futile attempt to enter the elevator.

'Sorry,' I said hesitatingly but she ignored it gracefully. I saw her rushing through the corridor towards the receptionist. She has never come to this floor before. Why is she in such a rush? I thought.

'God! That Senior Editor saved you. You should go and thank him,' suggested Bobby, sipping the fresh berry juice from a large tumbler.

'How do you know it's him and not her?' I asked and instantly realized my mistake.

'So, a thought crossed your mind? Must have been a long and lonely journey,' he snapped.

'What do you mean? What pleasure do you find in insulting me?'

'You see, I believe in telling the truth. I could say nice things about you. But that would be a blotch on my integrity, don't you think so?'

I threw my hands in the air in exasperation. Bobby was a winner by birth. I could not fight him. Finally, seeing my desperation and disappointment at the same time, he patted my back and said, 'You should thank your stars; if that proposal of yours had reached Peter, he would have thrown you out, leave alone promoting you.'

I nodded and secretly wished that someone came and told me the name of the Senior Editor. We decided to take the staircase in the hope of shedding some pounds.

'Careful,' Bobby grabbed my arm and pulled me.

And there again I missed the collision with the same lady by an inch. She glared at me from behind her specs. I felt the rage building up within her and folded my palms to offer my sincerest apologies.

'Bobby, I have to tell you something.' I scared him enough to knock him off his rocker.

'What?'

'I saw two lawyers representing Poilter Agency near our reception. The news has caused a stir and I am dying to know the details. Can you be of any help?'

'Of course, let us go to the ninth floor.'

At 4:30 PM, we came back to the seventh floor only to find most of the desks empty. It looked like everyone was enjoying Peter's day off! The last half-an-hour gave us too much to digest. The two lawyers were here to subpoena Adah Sharma who was the Senior Editor at NYT. But that was not all. Bobby took us to the machine room and told me to pretend photocopying some documents. The idea was to overhear the conversation happening in the next room. To our utter surprise, someone barged into the room moments after we started our act. The glistening drops of perspiration were evident on her forehead. The lady wore a mauve overcoat and she had given her hair the liberty to swish in the air. As she rummaged through the stack of files kept on the topmost shelf of a rusted rack, my attention diverted to the man who entered the same photocopy room along with Becky, another employee. They were discussing about the senior editor who had been asked to be presented before a jury for a miniscule article that had a more-than-expected impact on the company in question.

At 5:30 PM, Bobby and I left the NYT premises and headed back home. I did not have any energy left for having dinner outside. Though Bobby insisted earlier that we should celebrate the close shave, I postponed the celebration till the next day. While one part of me was sad that I would no longer be able to land the biggest client for Peter, the other part yearned to know more about the senior editor. No, I was not attracted to her. But yes, I was blown away by her audacious and alluring mindset. It takes immense contemplation to write an article with such brutal honesty. And she dared to stand tall and argue the toss.

Scarlet greeted me with a lot of hugs and kisses and I returned the favour by tossing an Oreo towards her. I spent the evening preparing rice-vege bowl for dinner. Sliced and sautéed capsicum, bell pepper and mushroom tossed over boiled rice with a spoonful of mint chutney and my mother's pickle- the perfect dinner for an evening like that. I switched on the TV and rested my eyes on Romedy Now that telecast The Proposal. I loved this movie. My mind wandered off to a distant land where I visualized the lady from the copy room in place of Sandra. Surprisingly, I was not in place of Ryan Reynolds. Instead, I only saw the girl whom I didn't know, busy with the chores in her office. Instantly I knew that the storm wouldn't settle so easily. I had to know more

about her. But whom to ask? Just then my phone rang and
I got my answer.

5

The Prolonged Learning Curve

My sister's flight was supposed to land in New York the next evening. As I recalled the timings of my meeting, I typed a message to Bobby asking him to pick up Nandita, my sister, from the airport. I couldn't go myself as I had a meeting scheduled with the editors and the designers.

In five minutes, my phone beeped and I knew it's Bobby.

Hey Bro,

Is your sister single? I don't mind picking her up and then, may be, going out on a date.

I smiled as I knew that he was not serious. I called him to tell the timings of the flight.

'Should I tell Sam that you have a date today?

'No, no, no, no. You'll get me killed. I was just kidding,' he pleaded.

I grinned from ear to ear. 'The flight will land at 5. Can you go?'

'I will try talking to Peter about leaving early from office.' Peter, the marketing head and our boss, had poor self-awareness; he bullied and stole credit of others. Nobody liked him. Unfortunately, I had to give a presentation before him and I knew he would not allow me to leave the office before he had made a mountain of a molehill and had humiliated me in front of several others. Thus, the only person who could save me from my younger sister's wrath was Bobby.

At 6:15 AM, I left for my office on my bicycle. I loved the idea of travelling on a bicycle. At least I did not have to worry about physical fitness. On my way to the New York Times, I picked a ham burger and decided to have breakfast in the office. I reached in another 10 minutes.

'Good Morning, Avyan!'

The sudden hoarse voice made my jump out of my skin. I hated Peter. I hated his way of scaring others. He sent out negative vibes that could sow the seeds of hopelessness and depression in anyone's mind. I was fortunate enough to be surviving in that place.

'Good Morning, Peter! How come you are here?'

'I can be anywhere. It is my way or the highway.'

'Well, that's not what I meant. Anyway, what time do you want the presentation to begin?'

'Only if you were prepared, I would have started it at this very moment.'

I had a sudden urge to smash his face with the glass vase kept on my table. But I brushed aside the flight of fancy and replied with due respect.

'For a change, I am well prepared. Let's go.'

Some days I amazed myself. Other days, I looked for my phone while I was talking on it. He stared at me as I collected the essentials. I could feel the heat radiation being thrown out from his eyes (yes, like Superman). He would have cursed me at that very moment. I waited for him to lead.

As I entered the conference room, a familiar fragrance made me lose my train of thought. I gathered myself up again and spread my utilities on the table. At the other end of the long table, I could see two women sitting and discussing something. Their backs were facing me but I could make out that they would not be easily convinced by my proposal. Spotting the cloud on the horizon, I braced myself for the battle. Come what may, I could not afford not panic nor zone out. That project was important and it was that one chance to leave an impression on Peter.

At 10:00 AM, I finally gulped down a glass of cold water. The presentation was over. Nobody had any questions nor any suggestions. Peter seemed impressed but he could turn the whole thing around and make it a can of worms. The women at the far end, the men in suits and the woman sitting by Peter's side- all seemed to have agreed with the budget and the marketing strategies. I tried to recall the names of all the attendees- Peter, Mr Rao, Mr Jacob, Ms Kyra, and Ms Jennifer. I was unable to recall the name of the woman who sat beside Peter. She wore glasses and her hair was tied in a bun with the help of a golden clip, the sparkle of which perturbed my fluent speaking skills. She was delightful to look at. But who was she? I had seen her whispering something in Peter's pointed and alien ears. Was she making fun of my accent?

I reached back to my cabin, took off my blazer and let the chill of the wind cool down my anxiety. Time passed quickly. At 8:45 PM, I pinged Bobby and asked about my sister's arrival.

'Yes, she is with me. She wanted to shop and so I have brought her to the Nike store. Where are you? How was your meeting?'

'Man, it was something. I am on my way home. Can you keep her company for another 20 minutes?'

'Yes, sure. Come soon.'

Quick as a wink, I scooted out from my cabin and cycled homewards. Nandita was extremely eccentric just like me; she took every little thing very seriously. I was scared for Bobby. If he would project his foolish side, Nandita would not even think twice before slapping him.

At 9:10 PM, I reached the Nike store only to find Bobby missing. When I gestured to Nandita, she pointed towards the alleyway. I walked towards the glass wall and saw Bobby busy on phone. Sobbing and wiping the tears with his folded sleeve, he looked pathetic. It took less than a fraction of a second to guess the situation. It was Sam. She must have said something which had made Bobby lose control. We waited for him to finish and meanwhile I narrated Bobby's story to my sister. She offered to sort out the matter but I safeguarded the territory before the bomb decided to explode itself.

Eventually, I bid goodbye to Bobby and took my sister home after having dinner at Carmine's.

I stayed up till 12 even though I knew that I had office the next day. Nandita was busy showing me all the gifts she had brought for me from India. Meanwhile I messaged Bobby to ask if everything was fine. He didn't reply for ten minutes. I became worried. But then my phone beeped. Nandita gave me another glare. I shrugged my shoulders as if nothing had happened. I read the message.

Sam is mad at me. I don't know how and when she saw me with Nandita. She thinks I am not upgrading my card because I am cheating on her. Man, I can't handle it anymore. But whenever I think of my life without her, I see the void.

I felt bad for him and typed an immediate response.

Don't worry, Bob. Don't stress. We will figure something out. I will talk to Sam and explain everything. I am positive that she will believe you once you talk to her properly and that too, face to face.

'Mummy has sent this pickle for you.'

'Really,' I jumped with excitement. I loved the garlic pickle my mother made. Some things in life don't change. For me. those are homemade food and my mother's voice. Those were equivalent to the air I breathed.

'What else have you brought?'

'Dad has sent these Adidas shoes for you.'

My heart skipped a beat.

My mind was still.

I didn't move.

'Avyan, what happened to you now?'

I didn't answer. Her name was Adah. I remembered. I felt euphoric. The woman who had caught my attention in the meeting was Adah, Adah Sharma, the Senior Editor. I couldn't forget her face. I looked flushed. It all came running back to my mind. Adah was the woman in the beige coat, she was the one who had entered the copy room, she was the one whom I had angered when I had missed colliding with her by an inch. All that while, she was right before my eyes yet I was such a half-wit not to be able to connect the dots. Embarrassed at my sudden look, I immediately concealed my emotions behind a fake concern.

'So, how is your new job?' I tried my luck and succeeded.

Nandita didn't notice the redness on my face. 'It's good. This new project might open new doors for me. Anyway, when will you introduce me to the editor of your newspaper?'

I had almost forgotten why Nandita had come there. She had become a part of a new project in which she had to do internship under the mentorship of a well-known editor. My little devil had earned a master's degree in journalism. She wanted to become an editor. But she realized late that it was not a cakewalk. Since I was pretty confident about my contacts in my office, I had assured her an internship at NYT. Luckily, her application had got selected without even my intervention. That was last week. The editing staff had called her for an interview. I was a benefit in disguise for my sister, for the next day I was going to take her to Susan, my friend. I thought she would easily get the internship when Susan would see her determination and quality of work.

'We will go to Susan tomorrow. She is the editor-in-chief. I think she'll be the right person to guide you. Be ready by 6.'

'Sure.'

As I rose from the cushioned chair and stretched my arms and legs, my sister's next statement made me raise my eyebrows.

'By the way, I saw the look on your face when I mentioned Adidas. Why did you look so rosy?'

'Rosy? Me? No way! You have lost your mind.'

She hit me with the cushion lying beside her and I did the same to return the favour. Even though she was five years younger, she behaved as if she was my mother- dictatorial and demanding. My mother was behind my sister to get married. Probably, my decision to remain single had made her hysterical. But Nandita was clever. She had promised mother that she would get married after she accomplishes her dream of becoming an editor. She was taking it slow, very slow.

I opened the loft and pulled out the extra mattress that I had bought when I had come to the city for the interview and had stayed with Bobby. A white bedsheet and a thin pillow were what I needed to sleep. Gesturing Nandita to claim the bed, I spread my mattress next to Scarlet's soft hideout. I put my thumb and my forefinger in my mouth to emit a whistling sound and that indicated Scarlet that it was time for bed. She was ecstatic to see me near her bed. She came running towards me and jumped on my chest. Though it was a little painful, I enjoyed every bit of her love. I caressed her face and loaded her with kisses. Nandita shouted from inside- Go to sleep, you two. And we both followed.

I stretched my arm to switch off the lamp and set an alarm for the next day. The moment I closed my eyes, I started remembering all the tiny details that could help me put together the pieces of the jigsaw puzzle- Adah. I could hear the tapping of the table with her long nails that had pink colour on them. I remembered the shine of her golden clip, the red glasses that kept sliding on her nose. The midnight moonshine played hide and seek with the clouds. The room was warm and Scarlet's face was on my stomach. That day, I didn't feel satisfied. There was something amiss. I tried harder. But I didn't know what I was thinking. I didn't know what I was looking for.

I decided to leave the pieces of puzzle as they were. I started feeling lighter. But soon the feeling faded away. I struggled for a while and then I succumbed.

6

As Fidgety as A Child

The next day in the office was bad and sad as well. There was a power cut in the morning and I couldn't iron my shirt. Consequently, I had to put on tawdry clothes. Had I suddenly become very conscious of myself? I followed my usual chores of picking up my breakfast and then heading straight to the office. I had to meet Bobby. He had called just in time the day before. Instantly I knew that he could help me know more about Adah. After all, he was an acquaintance of Becky's because both of them hailed from Pittsburgh. Becky worked with the editors. So, she was our best shot. Breathing a sigh of relief, I rushed to his place and pinched his cheek. Caught unawares, he punched me hard in my stomach.

'What's your problem, dude? Why have you been behaving differently lately?' He shot at me.

'I'm sorry, but I felt like squeezing your cheeks today!' I defended myself.

'Okay! What do you want?'

'For how long have you known Becky?' I asked coyly.

'Dude, seriously? Becky? She is out of your league. She wouldn't care even if you jumped off this floor!'

'No bro. It's not about Becky. It's about her friend, Adah.'

It felt as if my words had knocked every wisp of air from Bobby's lungs.

'And why on Earth would you be looking for more information about Adah?'

'Simply!'

Bobby knew that it was a matter of the heart. Following the bro code religiously, he didn't interrogate me anymore and gestured to meet him in the cafeteria. I followed his lead and the next thing I did was order a cappuccino and a croissant.

'Are you in love, my boy?' Bobby probed.

'No! What rubbish! I just want to know more about Adah,' I interjected.

'Ha! I know, I know. Where is Nandita? Wasn't she supposed to come along?'

'She came with me and I introduced her to Susan. I think she is still with Susan. She will text me once she leaves.'

'Leave the office, you mean?'

'Nah! She is leaving my apartment and shifting with our cousin. Both of them love each other like crazy. Nandita thinks she cannot tolerate my tantrums for long! How wrong is that!'

'She is right, you know. I should be awarded for bearing you for so long!'

I glared at Bobby. He took out his phone the very next moment and dialled someone's number. I thought he had called Becky. Like a dog with two tails, I waited.

'Hey, what's up? How is it going? How is your foot now?' asked Bobby.

I wondered what had gone wrong with Becky's foot. Poor girl! What Bobby said next made me realize that I had got hold of the wrong end of the stick. He wasn't talking to Becky. He was talking to Tanny Cole. Yes, Tanny Cole out of all the people in the world! He blabbered for another fifteen minutes and then came to the point. He asked her about working with Adah on a new article. I wondered what had gone into his head for trying to retrieve information via a third person. But knowing how he would react to my interference, I decided to keep my opinions to myself and wait till he finished the call.

'Why did you call Cole?' I puzzled.

'Listen to me, Cole works as a Publishing Product Designer. She is the best but she has her ways of doing things. Two years back, Cole and Adah worked on one of the print editions of the New York Times. People were jealous of their combination. It was lethal. They gelled so well that distractions were no longer a part of their routine. That issue recorded the highest sales figures. Consequently, when Dev Prakash, the Designing head, praised Cole and Adah, Peter felt left out. Even though he had done the bare minimum for the publicity and promotions, he assumed that an iota of credit will fall in his kitty too. Such a fool he was! And that is the reason he hates Cole so much.' Bobby finished.

'Then why did Tanny leave the job?'

'No brownie points for guessing.'

'Oh no! She was fired. How did Peter manage to do that?'

'He didn't. Dev did. Peter just had to become a little brown-noser.'

'No! You are joking, aren't you?' I sputtered.

'No! It's true. Hence, I called Cole to see if she would grab the opportunity and agree to meet with us.'

'How is meeting with Cole helpful in my case?'

'Sometimes I wonder what if your brains were dynamite- there wouldn't be enough to blow your hat off!'

'Seriously, do you want to start again?' I groused.

'What? You still didn't get it?'

'No. Of course, I didn't get it,' I grunted.

'Oh my God! Avy, if Cole decided to work with Adah, she would ask us to fix a meeting. You can get a direct chance to talk with Adah and set up a meeting for which she will be forever grateful. Isn't this the most brilliant idea ever?'

I couldn't argue the toss. Bobby was intelligent and I knew he was right. Rather than opting for a cheesy way to talk to Adah, this seemed and sounded more professional and more dignified. So, with Becky out of the picture, Cole was our new bait and Adah was the prey- or that's how Bobby put it.

We returned to the salt mines and spent another hour or so working on various proposals, budget plans and several presentations. While I was browsing through the fifth file, it suddenly struck me that I had forgotten to ask Bobby the most important question- did Cole agree?

'Yes, of course. How could she turn down my offer?' Bobby boasted.

'So, now what?'

'So, now you will go to the ninth floor tomorrow and speak with Adah. Just remember not to sound very desperate. I have known Adah to be a very reserved person and I don't think she encourages or entertains such sleazy moves.'

'Aye, aye, captain!'

After having a good night's sleep, I got up the next morning, showered Scarlet with a large number of kisses. I was happy. As the sunbeam peeped through the mustard curtains, the small round mirror on the wall sparkled. Magical as it seemed, I liked my own company. Sometimes you just need to be alone, that's okay. It doesn't mean anything is wrong in your life. Sometimes you need the space to search for your soul, recover, rethink, rest and just be. You don't need to apologize for needing or taking this space; it is a part of what makes you happy and healthy. That was my space- my moment to enjoy life and just be. That was the most perfect moment and I was pretty much confident that talking to Adah would further make that moment beautiful.

I got ready and cycled to my office. Reaching before time, I called up Bobby to check where he was. As expected, he was already at his desk. As I went closer, he waved a long piece of paper and smiled from ear to ear. His look scared me.

'Why are you smiling?' I asked.

'Yesterday night, I spent four hours in scripting the conversation that you would have with Adah,' he declared.

'What nonsense! I know what I have to say. Why do you have to play the fool always?' I deadpanned.

'What? If you know everything, then tell me the headline of the news piece on which Adah and Cole worked together. Tell me the month of publication. And also tell me…'

'Okay, okay, I am sorry. Show me what you've got,' I surrendered.

The six-page long script was more like a movie script. If only one could add songs and a few explicit scenes, it could have been used to make one all-time hit motion picture starring Adah and me. I laughed at my pointless thinking!

The snap of Bobby's fingers broke my reverie. I took his leave and reached my desk. Spending only ten minutes to read the first side of the script, I called it quits because I wasn't born an actor. I couldn't remember the dialogues; I couldn't be expressive where Bobby had written 'give a scornful expression' or 'give a slant smile'. I decided to follow the course of nature and let things be.

After the lunch break, I headed straight to the ninth floor only to find out that Adah was not in her cubicle. Upon enquiring, I found out that she had gone to Murray Hill for a few days. She was working on a new article about college graduates and her research needed case studies. I couldn't help but sink into the chair I was sitting in. The very next moment Bobby informed me that Tanny Cole was available for a meeting in the next two days as after that she would be travelling to Yorkville on a new project. I could see my dreams, hopes and desires being crushed. The sunbeam showers made me break and quiver. Even the man in the poster seemed to be mocking at my misery! On second thoughts, I also felt sad that I would miss a chance to see Adah for a few days.

After pack up, later in the evening, I decided to channelize all my energy in completing the pending work. Bobby had plans for the weekend and thus, just being me didn't help me any longer. Scarlet also denied the company at times. I thought that she also needed space for 'soul searching'. Aloof and alone, I began working on my laptop.

The next few days were spent in the 'wait' which not only seemed longer than usual but also made me restless. When Adah returned from her trip, I faced her like a happy camper. The journey till the ninth floor was easy. What was difficult was the part where I had to act formal and uninterested. I knocked at the glass door of her cabin and she gestured me to come in without even lifting her head. She was busy. My mind told me to turn back but my heart knew that I could brave that storm too.

'Hi, are you Adah?' I tried to pretend.

'Yes, and you are the man who cannot walk straight!' she commented.

'I am sorry for the other day. My mind was occupied elsewhere....' Before even I could finish, she cut me short.

'No, no, please! I didn't mean it that way. Come, have a seat.' She offered.

'I am Avyan. I work as an Advertising Manager, 7th floor,' I introduced.

'I know, Avyan. The other day you introduced yourself at the meeting. Remember?'

'Oh yes! How foolish of me!'

'What brings you here?' She was straight-forward. I had to tread carefully.

'Do you remember Tanny Cole? She has shown interest in working with you on a new article. Since you were out of town for a while, she contacted Bobby, my colleague, regarding the same.'

'Oh, how lovely! Yes, of course, Tanny is a sweetheart! I will be glad if I get a chance to work with her,' she chimed in.

Her nod made my day. We fixed up a meeting with Tanny and by default, Bobby and I were a part of that meeting as we were the catalytic force behind that reunion. We dined together the next evening. Though I didn't get to know much about Adah as the conversation was mainly restricted to formal topics, that meeting opened a doorway to heaven for me. I could meet or call Adah as we became more than just strangers.

For one and a half month, my friendship with Adah grew in leaps and bounds. Thanks to Bobby that he was there most of the times to fill the awkward silences with his silly jokes. Things were moving quickly, not in terms of my relationship with Adah but in terms of getting to know her better. I got to know that she believed in calling a spade a spade and didn't even think twice before speaking her mind. The only odd thing about that whole scenario was that she never spoke about her family nor her idea of love. However deftly Bobby brought up the topic of love or companionship, she dodged every single time.

Nevertheless, I knew that my heart had found a home that was much more comfortable than my studio apartment!

7

The Dubious Decision

Several weeks later

The never-ending thoughts of finding out a way to ask Adah to the Ball had made me go crazy. I had given a thought of writing a letter (not a Dear John letter for sure) but a proper formal one. I had also thought of sending a word through Bobby. Like a Bollywood fanatic, I even thought of sending Scarlet with a ribboned note attached to her collar. But that would have been too much! Adah wasn't melodramatic; she was poised and unequivocal. Her pragmatic approach towards things was what drew me towards her. Brushing all the thoughts aside, I stepped out of my apartment. I plugged in my earphones and started playing Waltz for a Romance on my phone. I needed ideas. But before that, I needed a break. Jogging on the streets at about 9 in the night, I felt the fresh air brush against my face and its chillness kissed my lips.

After jogging for one hour which included eating another regular burger and packing fish and chips for my midnight meal, I sat down on a bench in a park near my building. The peace and calm of nature dandled me. I wished for a company- no, not Bobby's. Six months had just hurried by! So much had changed. I had understood my workaround in the city; Bobby had broken up with Sam; Nandita had gone back to Bangalore; Adah had become a regular columnist for NYC; my unrequited love for her had grown even more. But one person who hadn't changed at all was my little princess-Scarlet. I spent another fifteen minutes at the park and then headed back home. Both Scarlet and I followed our night drill and went to sleep hoping that the dream fairy would bless us with her magic wand that night.

I woke up startled by the sound of the drilling machine once again. Cursing the folly of those poor labourers, I searched for my phone; it was nowhere to be seen. Panicking a little (owing to human nature), I jumped out of the bed and exerted my knees to kneel. No, not under the bed- nor behind the side table. Did I leave it in the park? I remembered putting it on the bench but did not remember picking it back up. It was Deja Moo- I knew I had experienced this bullshit before!

There comes a time in life when one can spend minutes, hours, weeks or even months over-analysing a situation trying to put the pieces together, justifying what would have happened or one can just leave the pieces on the floor and move on. I didn't have a choice. The crowing cuckoo of the clock was enough to tell me that I would be late for work. I scampered like an overgrown puppy and paced towards the bathroom. With exactly 30 minutes in hand, I darted out on my bicycle and rushed past the parade of passers-by.

'Dude, what's wrong?' sputtered Bobby.

'My phone's missing. I couldn't find it in the apartment. Mike tried calling and it rang but no one picked it up,' I implored.

'What? Did you go anywhere yesterday? Did you forget your phone there?'

'I guess so. I had gone for a run.'

'Let's inform Peter and leave now. I think the guard would have found the phone if you had left it there,' assured Bobby.

Though I knew that the chance of finding my phone was minimal, I still found Bobby's words convincing.

We went and looked for Peter but could not find him. He was on leave. Unlucky us! We were a part of the greatest human tragedy- what we wanted we didn't have and what we had we didn't want. We left a message with Becky, Adah's friend, and went on a search patrol.

The phone wasn't in the park nor with the guard. We filed a complaint. Half an hour later, Bobby received a call. The unknown caller had my phone. She had found it on the bench in the same park. We rushed to get my phone back and eventually breathed a sigh of relief.

At 10:30 in the morning, after the circus of crazy adventure had come to a halt, I pinged Bobby on the chat and asked him to forward the details of the Waltz Ball. He was quick. The advertisement looked inviting.

Rotary NYC Reunion Ball

22nd of June

Intercontinental Hotel Reunion Ball

Grand Ballroom, 19:00

<u>*In the program:*</u>

Famous Strauss music

Opera stars' performance

Sumptuous dinner in best traditions of Vienna

Dance performances

Thoughts from last night revisited my mind and I zoned out for a little while.

'Avy, Avy- what's wrong with you?' Bobby jerked my shoulder.

'Nothing.' I let my smile answer his question, for my numb mind refused to frame a sentence. Suddenly the desire to see Adah took control over my senses. While I was making plans for the big proposal (metaphorically), Bobby shouted my name again only to disturb my sweet thoughts. I wanted Adah to be my partner but I did not have the guts to ask her out. To add to my misery, my introvert nature came in my way of love. I hadn't gotten to know anything more about her than her working hours, designation and her love for pastels. I didn't even know where she was born or brought up. I was pathetic.

A few hours later, when the work had clutched my mind completely, Bobby came running and panting towards my desk.

'What happened to you? Were you running a marathon?' I sweet-talked.

'What I am about to tell you will blow off your gasket!'

'Really? Try me!' I asserted.

'The marketeers and the printing people have applied extra brains and come up with this idea that instead of asking the employees to choose their partners for the ball, they will base the selection on an irrational game.'

'What rubbish!'

'Exactly my thoughts! The game requires all the Mademoiselles to write the colour of their gowns or dresses on a chit and submit to the organizers. All the guys will have a chance to choose a colour from the list displayed on the bulletin board and get a partner. The drill has already begun. Scores of ladies are gathering in the conference room on the 5th floor to give the colour of their dresses. And here we are- we don't even know if we will have a partner to go with!'

'What do we do now? Can we ask the ladies for the answer?'

'Of course, we can. But whom are you going to ask?'

'I don't know. Maybe I'll just skip the ball.'

'Don't be foolish. Give me some time- I'll figure something out.'

I knew he wouldn't be able to do anything. Bobby wasn't just cut out for things like that. Having Adah as my partner now seemed like a distant dream! My heart ached. The pathos in my life was enormous! I wanted to vanish.

After lunch, as Bobby and I walked towards the main gate of the building, I asked him if he had figured out anything. He stared at me with amazement.

'I forgot.'

Well, I knew about that, didn't I?

With shattered hopes of getting a partner, we decided to go to the 5th floor and register our names. Tim (one of the organizers) looked at us with surprise.

'Why did you both come so late? The registrations are almost over.' He informed.

'Well, is there anything you can do for us, Tim?' I beseeched.

'I think I can. There are still four colours left on the list. Take your pick.'

Mauve | Fire | Lapis | Walnut

My brain swirled with a lot of questions. I knew 'Fire' was a colour- a shade of yellow. But I hadn't heard of Merlon. I assumed 'walnut' to belong to the family of the Browns. I didn't know about Lapis too. Suddenly, my knowledge of colours seemed incomplete and I realized that proverbs are not just phrases. A little knowledge is a dangerous thing, isn't it?

'Just for the two of us,' Bobby danced with excitement, 'take your pick, Avy.'

I thought and thought. There was no certainty that one of these colours was Adah's answer. I didn't even have the slightest notion about her favourite colour. I decided to gamble.

'Mauve,' I said.

'Cool, I will go with Lapis then, though I don't know which colour is that.'

Tim registered our names and we returned to the salt mines.

That night I dreamt of Adah walking the ramp in a 'Mauve' coloured gown and smiling at me. When I tried to recall the colour, my mind hopped skipped and jumped and went on a holiday! Mauve was as vague as a mirage.

The good night's dream clubbed with a steaming cup of coffee helped me kickstart my new day. I had to talk to her.

It was then or never. Who knew I wouldn't be able to ace the test once again!

I left my apartment before my usual time and headed straight to the 7th floor of my office. Bobby was busy gossiping with his girlfriends from the nearby cubicles. I tapped his bum with my briefcase and signalled him to come to my cabin.

'Why now, man?' He whimpered.

'Just come,' I commanded.

I pulled out the brown teal drawer from its haven and took out the employee directory. Flipping the pages, I tried to mentally calculate the number of female employees in the office. The number was huge- 250! How would I even locate Adah in this crowd- I thought.

'Do you think you are smart, huh? I've met rocks that are smarter than you,' quipped Bobby.

I ignored his sarcasm and made him sit beside me on the stool.

'Look! There are 250 female employees here. How will we figure out who will wear Mauve or Lapis coloured gown?'

'Hold on. Is this what you have been thinking all this while? And I thought you were happy that we have at least found the partners. What's going on?' He provoked.

'Nothing. I was just wondering whether the editors will come to the Ball or not!'

'And why only the Editors?'

'Simply asked. Nothing serious, I promise.'

'Liar! Look your pant is on fire.' He joked.

I pressed my lips in frustration after hearing his lame taunt. Guessing the follow-up, he chose to ignore and replied in the affirmation that ladies from all the departments would be a part of the Ball Dance. I felt relieved. I did not have the guts to share my feelings with Bobby. He didn't even know how I met Adah and his questioning machine would put me in a black mood for sure.

Later that day while packing up work, I thought of what I would do at home. It was 5 in the evening and I was leaving early as the workload was less. Moreover, Peter was absent. Bobby had some proposals to be proofread and thus, he decided to stay for another hour. I decided to spend some cosy time with Scarlet and bathe her too. She loved jumping around the house when wet! Although that would lead to the transformation of the house into a dirty mess, yet I preferred that option over anything. As I came out of the glass door, I felt something gooey under my shoe. There was a colossal amount of black on the floor. I looked around for the culprit but there was no one. And then I saw one of the helpers coming my way with wet wipes.

'What was dropped here?' I asked.

He took out a mascara bottle from his apron and presented before me. 'Madam slipped and dropped this. I hope she didn't get hurt.'

I nodded showing concern and made my way to the main gate. Who would carry mascara to work? But Nandita also carries a small make-up kit, doesn't she? Are all girls like this? I wondered.

Who knew that this black mascara belonged to Adah? I got to know that when I saw her on the other side of the office standing with Becky and laughing off the black spots on her pink top. Her demure self-demanded to be seen. Though she did not like speaking much with everyone, her words compensated well. I had taken an instant liking to the columns she wrote in the New York Times. Her charming wit and everlasting sense of humour disarmed the audience instantly. It felt like she used a magic wand to write; each word weighed to precision. It hooked the readers. When the company had used her editing skills enough, they finally decided to promote her to the post of a regular columnist last month. Jumping on the bandwagon, Adah also didn't leave any stone unturned to prove herself. Becky once told me that this was Adah's dream job- writing for the New York Times. But I didn't know anything more. I knew more about Becky than I knew about Adah. And that pained my heart.

8

Making Headway

Finally, the D day arrived. All contemplation and statistical analysis had proved out to be unprofitable. I had given up the idea of finding out our partners. On a slightly surprising note, Bobby didn't quite seem perturbed by the thought of attending the Ball with a stranger. It's God's way of telling me to move on- he kept saying.

With Adah not in the picture anymore, the desire of being a part of the Ball had died down. I would rather sulk in my cabin than attend the dance. I had bought a new tuxedo with a peaked lapel to give a more formal appeal. Also, I preferred a traditional look. Keeping my clothes in airtight packets, I ensured that Scarlet's fur was light years away from it. Bobby had decided to come over to my place and get ready. I did not deny, for I needed company more than anything else. It took me a whole 15 minutes to make Scarlet comfortable in Bobby's company. She despised him owing to his flaky manners. He would try annoying her with a toy that he assumed was liked by her. How many times had I told Bobby that Scarlet hates squeaking sounds! Every time I forgot that he was as scatter-brained as an old lady. And so, he wouldn't remember any of it.

As the clock struck 5:45 PM, we rose from the rug and started running for the usual chores. Bobby took off his shirt and went straight into the bathroom.

'Why the hell do you want to bathe now? I objected.

'If you don't want a sarcastic answer, don't ask a stupid question,' retorted Bobby.

'What's so stupid in this? You took off your shirt and now you have occupied the bathroom. Where should I get ready?'

'Cranky! Why do you fuss over things like you are a small child? I like washing my face in the bathroom.'

I felt relieved.

We were ready, dressed to the nines, by 6:15 PM. The venue was a little farther from my place and it would have taken us half an hour to reach there. We hired a taxi and set out on this forlorn adventure.

My eyes were at stalk when I entered the ballroom. 7200 square feet with a dramatic 16' ceiling, the ballroom was appointed with magnificent chandeliers. The crème coloured palette was sure to compliment your chosen colour. A minute inside the ballroom, my eyes were so restless that I could not decide where to focus. There were so many details. The hall was a tribute to excellence. We were not early but just in time to witness the entry of some of the most beautiful ladies of New York. One by one, in their gilded opulence, the ladies walked down the stairs so gracefully that it was impossible to recollect their dweeb look from the office. Since most of the men already knew who their partner was, they went forward to escort their date to the dance floor. Bobby and I were as clueless as a camel which had inexplicably found itself at the North Pole. But as expected, Bobby initiated.

'Why do you look so confused?' He asked.

'So, do you.'

'I don't. I am just eager to meet her. Aren't you?

'Yes, I am. But how am I going to recognize her?'

'You don't have to. She would have already found out who her partner for the evening is. Women here are more upfront than men.'

'Still, isn't this behaviour normal?'

'Not at all. Peanut prizes inspire monkey contestants. Remember that you are unique.'

'Just as everyone else,' I concluded.

Bobby heaved a sigh of vexation. He knew his words of wisdom could not convince me. Just then the music started playing and the host welcomed us all. He seemed so fresh and excited. His partner looked older than him. Nevertheless, they connected well with the guests.

'Look! She's also here,' Bobby jerked my shoulder breaking into my reverie.

'Who?'

But he didn't answer. I had to turn and look for myself. Lo and behold, Adah walked down the stairs in a purple (ish) evening gown. Augmenting her femininity, her flowing gown dazzled my eyes. With a low décolletage, long bouffant skirt and a constricted bodice, I could not help but drool over her looks. She was beautiful. Her bard arms were busy in their chores- one holding the gown and helping her walk and the other sliding her spectacles above her nose time and again. Her gown was layered with swags and puffs and smaller details consisted of flowers, lace, rosettes and ribbons. I was expecting one of the gentlemen to go forward and offer a hand to her. But none came in sight. Before even I could conclude, Adah walked up to me making me weak in my knees.

'Hi…' I stammered.

'Good Evening.'

'Good Evening,' I bowed correcting my manners.

I felt like I was on cloud nine. Sure that I had chosen Adah as my partner, I started rehearsing the dance steps in my mind.

'Where is Bobby?' she asked dropping a bombshell on my trance.

'Why do you ask?'

'He is my partner,' she explained.

In the fit of rage, I would have killed Bobby right at that instant. He, too, looked surprised. I gestured towards him and stepped aside. Only if I had chosen Lapis instead of Mauve!

'I think your partner is searching for you upstairs,' Adah told me.

'But isn't she supposed to come here?'

She shrugged her shoulders and began her small talk with Bobby.

'Who is my partner? Do you know her?' I interrupted.

'Of course! It's Brenda!'

I felt the earth shake below me. Gradually, I would succumb into the tiny soil particles and never come back.

'Dude, there is a difference between having an open mind and having holes in one's head. Things would have been better had you given Brenda a chance.' I knew Bobby was the happiest person at that moment. And I could see that on his face that was glowing under the helium lights. On the contrary, my cheeks were flushed with rage and disgust. Moments later, Brenda came up to me and taunted, 'Opinions are like assholes and everybody has got one.' I smiled in return.

The evening couldn't have been more embarrassing. After dancing to the tunes of the Strauss music and tolerating the Opera show, it was time for the ball dance.

With my eyes hooked on Adah, I managed to place my left hand gently on Brenda's waist. She twitched. That unhinged me. Bobby, as happy as Larry, had decided to beat his gums. His incessant chattering didn't seem to bother Adah and that annoyed me more. Meanwhile, noticing my discomfort, Brenda took the initiative of smoothening the wrinkles in our (professional) relationship.

'Why are you so edgy?' she queried.

'No, not I. I am fine. I am,' my stammering gave away the plot.

'I can see that. Come on now, tell me what's wrong. Is it because I am your partner?'

'No, no. It is nothing like this. It's is just that I don't know how to dance,' I lied.

'Liar! Let's begin again. Why don't you introduce yourself to me?'

'I am Avyan. I work with Bobby and …'

Before even I could finish my introduction, she cut me short and interrupted, 'Not again! Please don't be a bore. Tell me what you like.'

'I like dogs. I have one at home. Her name is Scarlet,'

'More of your conversation would infect my brain,' she muttered under her breath.

'What did you say?' I challenged though I wasn't sure of what she said.

'Nothing. I need a drink- will be right back,' saying this she sprinted away.

Like a lone ranger, I stood my ground and waited for Brenda to return. That never happened. I didn't understand what offended her. A few minutes later when Bobby saw me thumping the ground aimlessly, he hurried towards me.

'What did you do now? Where is Brenda?' he asked.

'She just left to get a drink and never came back,' I said. Bobby urged me to re-tell the entire conversation I had with Brenda and then he revealed that I had fallen at the first hurdle of the Ball dance. While Brenda was trying to get into the mood and get naughty, I played the fool and shooed her away (unintentionally though). Remorse took over the place that sadness had occupied in my heart. As I turned back to go to the counter and drink away the fateful night, I felt a tap on my shoulder.

'Hi…'

'Hi, how come you are here?' I fumbled. It was Adah.

'Bobby just went to get the drinks and he told me that you wanted to talk to me about the Poilter Agency article,' she finished.

'Me? Poilter Agency?' I sounded unsure.

And then it struck me. My dearest friend had proved out to be the best wingman I could have wished for!

'Yes, yes about that. Just before reading your article about the Agency, I was planning on submitting a proposal to Peter about landing Poilter Agency as our prime client. Your article saved me from public humiliation,' I said in one breath.

'But how did you know that I had written that piece?'

'We came to your floor to enquire…'

'That's the reason you were there that day.'

Couldn't I keep my emotions in control? Why did I have to sound so excited! She had caught me off guard. The cat was out of the bag.

'Not really. We had gone to the ninth floor to photocopy some documents. You know how our floor is always so crowded and disorganized as well!' Bobby defended. I wondered what I would have done without this idiot!

'Oh, I am glad I could be of some help to you.' Adah smiled.

Just then the music changed course and the pulsating beats relaxed the knots of the muscles at the side of my jaw. As I started tapping my feet on the ground, Bobby understood the cue.

'I have to make an urgent call. It's is my mother. Why don't you both start dancing till then?' He didn't wait for Adah's response. He took her hand and placed it in mine. She couldn't refuse. Not that she couldn't resist my charm but because she deemed it necessary to be polite and courteous.

That time the music sounded mellifluous and time seemed to slow down. I could make every move of mine with precision. She was beautiful and we were perfect together. We didn't speak; we just followed the beats and our feet moved coherently.

'You seem to know this dance. That's so nice. I think I have two left feet.' She admitted.

'Are you kidding me? You are such a good dancer. Every move of yours is perfect. You are just being humble,' I said with my cheeks redder than the cherries.

'Not at all. Anyway, what are your plans now? Will you still work in NYT?'

Knowing fairly well that Adah didn't like long and monotonous conversations, I briefly told her about how I wished to continue there because I wanted more exposure before changing the job. She nodded in agreement. After all, she had been a part of the editorial team even though she was worth a lot more. Often we are forced to do things that might seem like a hurdle at first. Gradually we realize that those hurdles are, in reality, the stepping stones to something great. We spent the rest of the evening chatting about our jobs, Scarlet and Bobby at large. She didn't reveal much about herself. I just got to know that she was not docile. As far as her rough first impression was concerned, I understood that she carried a lot of baggage. Whenever I would talk about my family back in India, she would choke for a minute and then regain her composure and deftly change the topic. I learnt that she had a sister who lived in the same city but seldom visited her. I also understood that she disliked dogs or cats or any animals for that matter. She adored plants and liked having a mini garden in her rented apartment in West 45th street.

A little later, Bobby came back.

'How is it going, people?' he asked in a loud voice.

'It's going great, Bobby. I am glad I met Avyan. He is so genial and quite interesting, I must say.'

Bobby and I returned home by 11 PM. I was in love and Bobby knew that. He decided to leave me in the hands of my imagination. Scarlet was already there to comfort me and give me company. I was looking forward to the next day as it promised a new friendship and maybe, a new bond.

9

A Flicker of Hope

Tip-toeing my way into the kitchen, I switched on the light only to find the ubiquitous Scarlet already waiting for me there. How did she know? I had ensured to walk so stealthily! Nevertheless, I focussed on my mission to find something sweet in the refrigerator. Scarlet, too, seemed to be on a similar mission. Upon finding a single slice of pastry from last light, we engaged in an unspoken battle about who would get to eat it. Scarlet won, for her puppy eyes did the trick on me.

As I turned and rolled on the bed after every five minutes, images from the Ball flashed before my eyes. I wanted to talk to Adah about so many things. Did she have a family back in India? Why didn't she speak with her sister more often? How was she as a child? Had she been an introvert right from her childhood days? Was she in a relationship? I dreaded the answer to the last question but something in my heart told me that she was not seeing anyone at the moment. I decided to go with my gut feeling, for that was the best option.

The next day, having decided to paint the town red, I scurried to the seventh floor. I looked for my friend but could not find him. I asked a few people but nobody knew anything about him. Just then I felt a tap on my shoulder.

'What's up with you? Missing someone? A cumberground?' queried Peter.

'That's quite rude, Peter. You cannot address a person using this word. Bobby works day and night to add to the glory of this company and you are…'

'Did I say I was talking about Bobby? Oh, I don't think so. I was calling you cumbersome- always spending time on the least important things,' Peter snorted.

'What? What do you mean?'

'Forget it. How is the progress on the Niagara USA Wine Festival?'

'I am working on it. However, I think we can use an article on food and social media- how these two are related- to promote restaurants,' I suggested.

'And you are going to write that article for me and land us all in trouble, isn't it?'

'No, not at all. Why would I write? I know a person who might just be the perfect choice for this. If you give the green signal, I can arrange for a nicely written article and then I can work on the budget design and marketing proposal. Moe's Southwest Grill, Rowland's Bar and Grill and a few other barbeque restaurants have sent a request seeking promotions. They are ready to pay up,' I insisted.

'But if we have to promote them, why can't we just give them a little space in the paper and print the adds directly?'

'Because the world is changing and purpose and intention are everything. As long as we have the purpose of doing something, we can get the attention of the customers. When purpose fails, the advertisements just become a source of entertainment and to be very honest, wastage of space as well,' I defended.

Something stirred in Peter's peanut-sized brain. He didn't argue for the sake of arguing any more. I realized that Adah's influence was aiding me in coming across as spontaneous and intelligent. Or maybe it was Bobby's influence. I still preferred to give Adah all the credits though!

'Well, I can't say if your idea is fool-proof. You need to show me the article first. Then I will take a call,' Peter concluded and turned his back on me.

'Sure, I will.' I snickered.

Bobby had taken a day off as he had gone to meet Sam. No, they were not going to reconcile. They wanted to meet to exchange the gifts that they had given each other. As illogical as it sounded, it was something that Bobby felt was important to do- to get rid of the memories. Even if Sam wasn't hurt after the break up, Bobby still had an abyss left in his heart. He held Sam very dear. Although he had been advocating the relevance of moving on, I knew for a fact that it wasn't easy for him. Sometimes the idea of love sounded so unreal but whenever I saw Adah, I knew that she could change my perspective forever.

That day, I decided to enter the battlefield at my own risk. I reached the ninth floor and asked Becky if Adah was in her cabin. Becky nodded, I proceeded and knocked at the mirror-like glass door.

'Oh hi, Avyan, please come,' Adah greeted politely. She was dressed in a lime coloured A-line dress and a denim jacket that had a small flower patch at the very edge. She had let her hair loose and the spectacles, like always, kept sliding down her nose.

'How come you are here?' she asked.

'Actually, I have come here to ask you a favour,' I faltered.

'Of course, go on.'

'Well, while I was operating Facebook yesterday, I came across a post that included a lot of food pictures. As delicious as it seemed, I also learnt that as soon as I saw the pictures, I searched for the source and landed on the website of the restaurant. That was my light bulb moment. Since I have been getting requests from various restaurants regarding promotions and advertisements, I thought of promoting their brand with a purpose- an article with an advertisement. What do you think?'

'I still didn't understand what kind of article you are looking for.'

'An article on the relation between food and social media- a write up that illustrates the importance of social media and links that value with food value.'

'Aah, I am not saying that your idea is a flop, but I would be honest with you. I am not a very big fan of social media. I don't even use Facebook, Instagram or any other site. Don't you think I should not preach what I don't practise? I will come across as a hypocrite!'

'Yes,' I didn't know what else to say. But I got to know that Adah was not there on any form of social media and that was saddening. Soon realization dawned upon me and I understood how enslaved I was by the digital world. I was on Facebook, Instagram, Twitter, Tumble, Tinder and Pinterest too! Though I never shared any post or information on these sites, I revelled in my extraordinary advantage of keeping myself updated about others' life. At times, I felt my life was uninteresting but then very next moment Scarlet would cheer me up and I could sense the freedom that solitude brought along.

Adah had refused to write an article and I had to find out a way to involve her in the project so that I could talk to her. I left her cabin after the casual small talk because I could not come up with an idea. Later that day, I saw her leave the office building in a hurry while I was enjoying my evening snack by the food trailer. She was frantically rummaging through her bag but couldn't find the desired thing. I called out to her but my voice faded before it reached her ears.

'How was your day?' asked Bobby over the phone.

'Not that great. I tried asking Adah to write an article for promoting restaurants but she refused as she doesn't think she is the right person to write it.' I explained the context to Bobby and he agreed that Adah had been right in refusing to write.

'What to do now?' I asked worriedly.

'You write the article.'

'That's obvious now. But how do I talk to her or spend time with her?'

'You write the article first and then we will see. See to it that you complete writing it by tonight.'

The confidence in Bobby's voice did not make me question his command. I obliged and sat down to scribble on the old notepad. The night seemed long and I had pages to write.

After a lot of research and reading, I had almost finished typing the content needed. The article didn't have any scope of mistake, at least according to me. Bobby had asked me to send the article to him by email and I did the same before retiring to bed.

The morning rays of the glistening sun fell on my eyes. I was late. Peter would not leave this golden chance to affront me. Finishing my morning ablutions, I rushed to the office. I skipped breakfast but made sure I had fed Scarlet. I did not see Bobby in the office again. I called him instantly only to find out that the meeting with Sam didn't turn out to be great and hence, Bobby had extended his leave to another day. 'I need some time alone,' he said. And so, I let him be. The rest of the day was spent in tolerating Peter's banter and working under a lot of pressure. Post lunch, I decided to finish the pending work soon and leave for home. Just then, I received a call on the extension.

'Avyan, there is someone to meet you. Can you come to the reception area if you are free?' asked Sonali, the receptionist.

'Who is there?' I enquired.

'The senior editor from the 9th floor,'

'Yes, I will be there.'

I met Adah at reception. She handed me a stapled set of papers. The heading seemed familiar- The Influence of Social Media on Food! It was the article that I had written yesterday.

'How do you have a copy of this?' I faltered.

'I am sorry for having refused to write for you. Had I not done that; you wouldn't have hesitated to come to me for editing. '

'What?'

'Bobby emailed this to me yesterday saying that you needed my help but were sceptical about letting me know. And that's why Bobby sent me this. I have edited this; it had a lot many errors.'

'Errors? Like?'

'Grammatical errors- incorrect sentence structures and spelling errors. Maybe you were sleepy when you wrote this.'

'I guess so.' Bobby had set that entire scene up. I understood instantly. He had misspelt the words intentionally so that Adah would have something to correct. However, this time, he had let me down as Adah would forever think of me as someone who would make careless mistakes while typing. Not a very good impression indeed!

'When I read this article, I felt something was missing. If you can include some case studies about how people have got inspired to try new cuisines because of the posts they have read online, it would act as a cherry on the cake. I mean this is just a suggestion. You can ignore it if you want.'

'I am not saying that it is a bad idea but I think I will have to do some research before including such case studies. Thanks for the help though.' My eccentric self-answered trying to sound as polite as possible. I disliked when anyone pinpointed mistakes in my work when there weren't any. Already Adah had formed a wrong impression about my language skills and now she was giving me the advice to improve my content. That was too much!

'Sure. If you do consider this, do not send the copy to me for editing.'

My heart broke. Was she offended? What should I do to correct my mistake? Should I apologize? Before even I could apply brakes to my never-ending imagination, she tapped on my shoulder and said, 'I know you cannot make such grammatical errors. I knew the instant I saw the document. I thought of just playing along.'

'Damn! I am sorry. This must have been Bobby's idea.'

'It is alright. If you wanted to speak to me, you could have asked me directly. Do you want to meet over lunch tomorrow if you are free and discuss the case studies?'

'Of course, I would love that.'

Full of the joys of spring, I started counting my chickens before they had hatched.

10

Twist in the Wind

'Four people die minutes after eating a burger,' mumbled Adah, instantly stopping the tap dance that her nails were doing on the table.

'What?' I couldn't resist asking.

'I'm sorry. The first case study that I opened had this news highlighted. I think the customers did not check for the allergens and eventually met their fate.'

Astounded that I was, my tongue found difficulty in rolling. I could sense my failure. That was the first omen. Peter would never give me another chance and instead would get a chance to get back at me. Sensing my discomfort, Adah put her hand on my shoulder and tried consoling me. Even though her caress was a balm to my soul, the balm to my brooding mind was nowhere to be found! We spent many-a-days reading articles, extracting information from the library and taking public surveys. Bobby helped me prepare a questionnaire and shared it all across social media. Adah used word-of-mouth to inquire about the importance of social media in choosing food. I tried talking to my folks in India because Indians, food and internet are inseparable. And by the end of the second week, we were good to go. We had managed to find three case studies with facts that could convince a zombie also to publish the article. Now that Adah was well aware of the fact that my grammatical skills were exemplary, I had to think of another way to keep her involved in the project. So, I asked her help in changing simple words to the difficult ones. Like a good Samaritan, she helped me draft a masterpiece. Not only was I in love with her personality but I adored her intelligence as well. She had idioms at her fingertips. New words were like oxygen for her. Argus-eyed, she didn't leave any word unread. I pitched the article to Peter once it was ready.

'Who wrote it?' he asked raising his eyebrows.

'I did.'

'Come on, I don't believe it. What happened to your source?'

'That's all right if you don't believe me. My source bailed out on me. If you don't like it, I can always send it to another local magazine. Maybe it needs to be worked on a little more to be fit to be considered for NYT,' I joked.

But he took it very seriously.

'No, I didn't mean that. Well, leave it with me and I shall think over it.'

'Of course.'

The glint in Peter's eyes gave away the surprise that he desperately tried to hide behind his sardonic smile. I knew he was happy and his happiness meant my entry into the good books. Life seemed to have settled a bit. I had successfully convinced Peter to publish one of the articles that would land some very lucrative clients in our kitty, Adah was by my side and we could talk without any hesitation. Bobby was, as always, my friend in need, always indeed! And thus, I decided to spoil the broth that took too much of patience, mind and energy to boil. I decided to ruin everything, unintentionally.

After a few days of gossiping with Adah, I somehow felt the urge to confess my feelings for her. When I asked Bobby for his opinion, his response left a lump in my throat.

'I am planning to confess my love for Adah,' I said.

'I don't think that's the right decision, Avy,' he disagreed.

'Why?'

'Because I don't think she is ready yet.'

'But she does talk to me and she has often commented that she likes talking to me,' I tried persuading him.

'That's not love. Becky likes talking to me and spending time with me. Does that mean she loves me?' He disputed.

'You're joking, aren't you?' I cross-checked.

'I am not. She is not the type who would fancy a conversation of this kind. From what I know, she doesn't encourage men to make advances towards her. Just last year, Alan from the Training department approached her and asked her out. She was quick to make him realize that it was not love that he had for her.'

'Maybe she did that because we were meant to be together?'

'Now you are talking gibberish! You are pragmatic and know the rules of the world. Then why are you not using the big fat brain of yours now?'

'Because I love her and I do not want to lose her,' I explained.

'Avy, I can only advise you. The decision is yours because it is your life. I still believe that this is not the right time. You need to be patient.'

In the back of my mind, I knew that he was right. But my heart had another agenda.

I asked Adah to meet me the next day at Capizzi in the evening. Though she denied at first saying that she had some work, she had to agree when I told her that it was urgent. I did get a hint when she said no for meeting me at first. But this heart of mine, indeed!

'What would you like to have?' She asked me offering me the menu card.

'Whatever you say.'

'Okay. Two Iced teas and one Uovo Pizza- medium.' She moved her sling from the shoulder and opened the flap to take out her mobile. Bobby had once told me that if the girl uses her mobile while on a date, it indicates that she is bored. But was this a date? Shouldn't it be called a date? But I had to discuss business with her, then how was it a date? Brushing aside all the thoughts, I decided to initiate the conversation.

'So, Adah, what is your plan for Christmas? Are you travelling anywhere or will you stay here?'

'Avyan, we are not in school that we will have holidays. We have work and I cannot take leaves just because it is Christmas!'

'Yes, I meant to ask you your plans for the Christmas Eve. At least that day we wouldn't have to come!'

'Yes, that's true. At times, I feel that I should take a sabbatical and run away to a faraway land with no connectivity and no people as well.' Saying this, she laughed as if she had cracked the funniest joke.

'Shall I ask you something?'

'Yes, go ahead.'

'Why don't you ever go to India?'

'You have asked me this before and I am quite surprised that even though I didn't answer this before, you are still asking me the same thing.'

'Adah, I know that there is something that you always run from. And I believe it is something related to this. I will respect your choice of not telling me only if you tell me that you do not want to discuss this.' I acknowledged sensing her disquiet.

'Avyan, there are things that I do not wish to discuss. And now that I have made it very clear, I hope that you won't bring up this again.'

'Yes, I won't.'

We couldn't discuss anything else, for Adah made an excuse of work and left soon after. I had had my share of disappointment. She did not call or attend my call for the next few days. Unable to figure out the reason, I sought Bobby's help. At first, he chided me and cut the call. But then my persistent efforts did not go in vain. He suggested that we rope in Tanny Cole to get to know about Adah. But it wasn't as easy as it sounded. Why would Tanny agree to meet us and discuss her former colleague? What was the guarantee that she knew more about Adah than any of us? I didn't know the answer to any of those questions. But that was the only port in the storm. So, I decided to take refuge at that port!

Bobby tried to convince Tanny to meet us eventually. That was three days after the conception of the plan. I was scared. I didn't know what to say nor did I know how to begin. Hence, I had to take Bobby along. She sounded quite eager to meet Adah. The problem, however, was to tell Adah about this get-together.

'Hi, Avyan this side,' I said after she picked up my call.

'Hi. Why did you call at this hour? Is everything alright?' she asked.

'Yes, everything's fine. I just wanted to invite you for lunch tomorrow. But before you refuse, I would like to tell you that Bobby is meeting Tanny Cole tomorrow for some work and he suggested that you might want to catch up with Cole too.'

'Avyan, I wasn't going to say No. Why are you explaining so much?'

'Because we didn't meet after that dinner…'

'That's because I thought I had offended you. I had been thinking for days to come and apologize for my erratic behaviour but I could not muster the courage. Nevertheless, I will come tomorrow. Maybe we can chat after that and resolve the misunderstanding.'

My happiness knew no bounds yet again. But then Bobby's words echoed in my ears. Being patient was the only key. I had to wait for the right moment. I decided to find out all about Adah first and then think of conveying my feelings. Often when in love, we start believing that the past or the future doesn't matter. But that is not true, for often the actions are governed by either the past or the future. Adah had buried her past so deep within her heart that it did not let her fill her heart with new memories. I had heard about how everyone comes with baggage and they try their entire life to get rid of that baggage. Those who succeed, find new hope and new love in their life. Those who fail, remain miserable forever. At the drop of the hat, I reached the conclusion once again. For me, Adah had to get rid of her baggage and I took the oneness of helping her do so not knowing that it would be one of the biggest mistakes of my life.

The next day, Bobby began the conversation with Cole on a lighter note.

'How are you?' He asked.

'I am well. How is New York treating you both?'

'It is treating us quite well! I like the work culture here and the people are good too,' I tried sounding as genuine as possible.

'Oh, you need not lie. People here are only worried about themselves. No one cares. Seldom you find good friends but then people like Peter rip apart the friendship that you develop over the years.'

I liked her frankness. Everybody disliked Peter.

'How did you and Adah become such good friends?' I initiated the small talk.

'I think it was because of our love for the language. We met when there was a requirement of two writers for the new section in the paper and on the website. Most of the in-house writers did not want to be a part of it because this section required a critical eye and an open mind.'

'Which section was this?'

'The Op-ed section. This is the only section where the people are given the freedom to voice out what they feel. Writing articles for this section was not easy. Our pair clicked because when one would write about any issue, the other would critically analyze it and give honest feedback. But we would do that in such a way that it did not hurt much. Eventually, the response from the readers started seeming less rude and blunt. And that's how we gelled well with each other.'

Just then Adah joined us and we chatted for a bit. In the process, I got to know that Adah's parents lived in Delhi. She had a younger sister who lived in the same city but they weren't on speaking terms. I could not get to know the reason because Cole adroitly diverted the question. Just then I heard them speaking in whispers.

'I know, I know. So, what plans for tomorrow?' Cole asked excitedly.

'What plans! Nothing. I might take half a day off and spend time at home.' Adah responded rather wistfully.

'Come over to my place. We shall celebrate.' Cole offered.

'What's there to celebrate? I'll do the usual. Maybe buy an ice-cream and dinner too.'

'Are you going to call them?'

'I don't think so. It is awkward now. Calling them suddenly once a year and then falling silent- it bothers them as much as it bothers me. It is difficult for them as well, you know.'

I excused myself to get a lemonade and then thought. Plans for tomorrow- was it Adah's birthday the next day? Was she talking about calling her parents and then not being able to converse? But why did she want to spend time alone? I couldn't ask Cole; it would make me sound so frenzied. By the time I returned to the table, I saw them packing up.

'Thanks to both of you that I could spend some time with my long-lost friend,' Adah effused looking at Bobby and me.

'Mention not. We enjoyed your company too.' I added.

We went back to our houses after the formal goodbyes. Upon reaching my apartment, I found Scarlet hiding under the sofa. I tried to pull her out but as stubborn as she was, she growled showing her two teeth large and white. A little scared, I got up to get a piece of bacon from the fridge. Tempting her, I coaxed her to come out. And then by looking at her dry nose I knew she had a fever. I called up my mother looking for a home remedy and she told me to mix equal amounts of salt and sugar in water and make Scarlet drink it. I did that 5-6 times and made her sleep with me under the bed cover.

The night seemed longer than usual. As I waited for the morning rays of the sun, I also wondered what the day had in store.

I reached the office on time and started finishing the pending work. I wanted to meet Adah before she left the office. After two hours of rigorous work, I paced downstairs to the cafeteria to think about what to buy for her. And there I saw her. Adorned in a traditional salwar kameez, Adah looked like a goddess. Hair golden brown hair with streaks of red swayed left to right. Her nails were varnished with purple. Despite wearing high heels, her gait was flawless. She looked stunning! I raised my hand to say hi but realized that I was standing perpendicular to her and thus, she couldn't see me. She was headed to the food counter. I turned towards the door and scurried downstairs to buy fresh roses for her. I was sure that it was her birthday.

'Make one nice bouquet with yellow and red roses,' I urged the flower boy.

'Of course, sir. Is it for the one you love?' He asked.

'I guess so,' I answered.

'Then why yellow? Shall I make a bouquet with only red ones?'

'Oh yes, that would be fine,' I said almost instantly and then corrected my mistake by asking the boy to prepare a bouquet with a mix of yellow, red and purple flowers. I had to be patient. I couldn't let my heart win over my mind.

I carried the bouquet and entered the elevator. Just when the door was about to close, somebody put their shoe in between to halt the movement. It was Peter. My heart was fit to burst. I tried hiding the flowers behind my back unaware of the large mirror that reflected my foolishness, quite literally.

'What on Earth are you doing with flowers? It is not even my birthday,' rebuked Peter.

'These are for a friend,' I explained.

'Is it Bobby's birthday?'

'Bobby is not my only friend. I have other friends too,' I countered.

'Wasting office working hours, aren't you?'

'It's lunchtime, Peter.' I advocated my cause. But he wouldn't budge.

'You should reach your cabin before somebody drops a house on you.'

'I am headed there. You need not taunt me now and then,' I asserted.

'If you were twice as smart as you are, you would be half as smart as you think you would be,' he smirked. 'It was a joke! Take things lightly, Avy.'

I gulped down anger like one would gulp a sip of water on a dry throat. I ignored it. We got off at the seventh floor only to find Bobby chatting with Tanny Cole. I joined them and they both stole glances at the flowers and a small greeting card that hung right in the corner.

'Flowers? For whom?' asked Bobby.

'For Adah.'

'So, you know about it?' Asked Cole.

'Of course, I figured out yesterday only,' I beamed.

'She doesn't like gifts or surprises. I think you shouldn't go ahead with the flowers,' Cole advised.

'Even I have a gut feeling that you shouldn't give her these,' added Bobby.

'But why wouldn't a person want to celebrate such an occasion? It is not every day that your birthday comes, isn't it?' I asked, looking for approval.

'Birthday? Who said it is her birthday?' interjected Cole.

'What? Weren't you both talking about her plans for today? It's her birthday, isn't it?'

'No! My God! You don't know, do you? It is not her birthday. It is her anniversary- seventh anniversary,' Cole finished in one breath.

I felt the floor slipping away from beneath my feet. Bobby was left rooted to the spot. It wasn't rocket science for Cole to figure out what I had in my mind or rather in my heart. She was quick to offer me a glass of water before my emotions could drown the pain that I felt. Choking over water, I managed to ask just one question- 'Is she married?'

II

ADAH

11

A New Lease of Life

July 2004- University Campus

I woke with a start as the sound of my alarm tone hit my ears. It was seven in the morning. I knew I would end up embarrassing myself on the very first day of college. My mother wasn't there to wake me up and that's when I realized that I should have given a second thought about staying in the hostel. My family, as always, had been against my decision. But I stood my ground and explained how convenient it would become for me to attend extra classes by not having to use the metro for travelling. They did not understand. Still, they gave in to my request because of constant badgering. As the rays of the morning sun peeked through the ivory coloured curtains, I noticed the blankness on the walls. My room wasn't palatial. It was just enough to house one single bed, one study table and chair, one cupboard and one me! There was a big window facing the park where one could often spot a group of students studying, some of them whiling away time on the phone, some making friends and some tasting the first dose of love. I, however, had a different agenda. The path to my dream was crystal clear. I wanted to become a writer and write for the leading newspaper in the world.

Having opted for Journalism from Delhi University, I didn't have a choice to learn creative writing separately. My parents found my dream bizarre because they believed that 'intelligent' children could only become engineers or doctors. My younger sister didn't have anything to say. It didn't matter then but when she continued her habit even when she grew up, it bothered me a lot. I had only one close friend, Viha, from school. Her parents were quite opposite to my parents. They loved me like their own daughter. Viha and I spent most of our time after school playing basketball. While she dreamt of becoming an ace player of basketball one day, I dreamt of making my voice heard through my words. I got along with boys pretty well owing to basketball but when it came to adorning femininity, my efforts couldn't go ignored. Even though I wasn't impolite, I often found girls avoiding the conversation with me. Maybe it was so because I was academically good. Or maybe because boys often spoke to me with ease and comfort. Or maybe I just imagined so. Viha and I were separated after school as she went on to pursue Basketball on a professional level. I missed her often. Without her, life seemed strange and baffling.

The sudden knock on my door broke my reverie. I knew it was Suhana, my cubicle mate. She was my new found friend in college and I knew why she had come.

'Get ready, fast! We are already late. Do you want to miss the orientation programme?' she heaved.

'What happened to you? Why are you panting?' I asked.

'The life is out of bounds and I had to climb two flights of stairs to reach your room. Too much exercise for me, isn't it?'

'Yes, I know. Poor Suhana!' I laughed out loud.

While she waited in my room, I got ready. We walked amidst the tall brick buildings that overlooked the space of flowers. As the students passed by, we noticed how each one of them was dressed differently. That was the sheer joy of not having any dress code: one could wear as one pleased. The white lilies and the marigold embellished the otherwise plain walkway. With each step closer to our department, the churning in my stomach increased. I was nervous- nervous about making new friends, nervous about the syllabus, nervous about new life and nervous about being judged.

'Get in. You both are late to class. If you repeat this, you'll lose attendance for a day,' the professor warned.

'Sorry, sir.' I replied and walked towards the empty seat at the back. Suhana was pulled aside by one of the girls whom Suhana seemed to know. When I looked back at her, she gestured to me to carry on. And I anticipated my worst fears coming true.

'Who says sorry to the professors in college?' a voice came from behind me.

I turned and saw a head buried in the books. I chose not to reply because my life there had just begun. The class went on just fine with the professor asking each one of us to share our dreams and our action plan. When my turn came, I hesitated to share my dream but then Suhana gave me an encouraging smile and I spoke.

'I want to become a writer.'

'Shouldn't you be doing a different course for that?' asked my teacher with a baffled look.

'Uhh… I didn't know about any other courses. But I am sure that journalism will help me too.'

'Oh okay. I hope you are on the right path. My best wishes are with you.' The professor's concern was genuine and so was his wish. I wondered if I had made the right decision. But doesn't this happen often? When you decide something based on what your heart wants, the entire world decides to stand against you and tries to pull you down. It is then totally your choice- either to settle for the world as it is or work for the world as we want it to be. Some of the toughest decisions in life are backed by no support. Was this the toughest decision of my life already? I didn't know.

During the lunch break, Suhana and I headed to the cafeteria. Finding a seat in that closed hall seemed next to impossible.

'Let's first buy the coupons. What will you have?' vacillated Suhana.

'I don't know. Shall we take the meal- there is no rush there.' I sounded confident.

We took the coupons for the meal and started our lookout for a table. Once seated, we gossiped about the classes we had had and at the same time realized why the meal never invited more rush! The food was gross!

'What have they made?'

'God knows. If we eat this one more time, we won't be able to come to college anymore!' I said, disgusted by the taste.

'You could have tried fried rice instead. They taste better,' said the boy who sat right behind us. I glanced at him and almost instantly recognized the black striped shirt. He was the same boy who sat burying his head in the books. Feeling an unaccustomed lump in my throat, I tried to rebuke him for interrupting our conversation but no words came out of my mouth. While most people suffer from brain freeze, I experienced the moment of mouth freeze!

His eyes on the Margaret Atwood book that he was reading and his hands busy feeding his mouth, I couldn't help but appreciate his prowess to multitask! I turned back to face Suhana and at that very instant he stood up.

Tapping on my shoulder, he said, 'You forgot this on the table.'

Now annoyed, I looked at the green notebook that he produced from his brown leather bag. How could I be so careless!

'Oh, thank you! I didn't realize that I had forgotten my book.' And for the first time, I looked at his face. Brown eyes wearing reading glasses, freckles across the bridge of his nose, he was solidly built. Salt and pepper hair, ramrod straight and rock-jawed, his gunmetal eyes looked genuine. His shoulders mitred at a perfect ninety-degree angle. He didn't respond to my gratitude. Making way towards the exit, he excused himself and went past me.

Something happened at that moment. I wished I was a child again. Wouldn't it be easier to confess what I felt? That's the worst part of growing up, I guess. You are always prepared to fake your emotions, fake your expressions and fake your feelings! The uncanny feeling lasted for a while and I could not decipher why it was there in the first place.

After lunch, we hurried back to the class. An orientation session was scheduled in the second half. Some seniors had told Suhana that it was the most boring part of the college education. However, I wanted to get acquainted with the rules and regulations that would be followed for the next three years. As I entered the auditorium, my eyes frantically began searching for someone I didn't know. Overwhelmed by my stupidity, I tried to focus my attention on other details. The auditorium had a mix of people- some cool, some nervous, some confident and some very shy. I preferred not to categorize myself. Suhana pretended to be cool though. The programme began in another half an hour and it went on for ages or so it seemed. The director gave a speech to welcome us all and that was followed by a series of presentations explaining the dos and the don'ts in the campus. The last segment, however, sounded interesting. They called it 'Ice Breaking Session'.

'To make a formal acquaintance with you all, we have a session during which most of you might get a chance to come up on stage and introduce yourselves. This orientation is not only a chance for the first-year students but also for the seniors to get to know their juniors better. To begin with, we would like to call upon all the ladies wearing purple nail polish on stage.'

That was weird. Who would wear purple nail paint? And there were ten of them! After the formal introduction and a rendezvous session, the hosts moved on to the next criteria- all the ones who wore a black-striped shirt. I was struck dumb. I knew who would be up on stage. And he walked up to the stage!

'I am a writer. I like writing poetry,' he said and the auditorium was filled with cheers and applause.

'Why don't you recite something then?' said one.

And he began:

'As the hues of the mist fall upon the foggy window,

I see your chimaera in all its glory.

My fingers trace the outline of your body,

My soul searching for our new story!'

The lines were familiar. For a second, I thought that he had copied from the internet and then, within milliseconds, it struck me. Those were my lines! He must have read them in the green notebook. I stomped my foot on the ground and headed out. Fuming in anger, I decided to confront the crook the next day. But the confrontation couldn't be delayed, for the crook came running behind me.

'I am sorry for using your lines,' he said, panting heavily.

'What's the use of an apology after the damage has been done?' I snapped.

'Well, for starters, I am accepting my mistake and trying to make amends.'

'And how do you plan on doing that? By stealing another verse of mine?'

'No, of course not! Let me explain, please.'

I didn't respond. I wanted to get away from that place as soon as possible. I headed back to my hostel and spent the rest of the day within the four white walls. Just then I received a message from an unknown number. Impulsive that I was, I concluded and assumed that it was from that same boy. I wondered how he managed to get my number and drafted a message in my mind rebuking him for his audacity.

Attendance register not signed. Kindly come to the auditorium to mark your presence for the orientation programme.

The message was from the admin staff. I had forgotten that life was more about attendance than about anything else. I got up in a jiffy, put on a shrug over the loose t-shirt that I was wearing and headed out. In less than ten minutes, I reached the building. I saw Suhana chatting with some girls-girls who looked like nerds. I motioned my hand asking her to come but she signalled me to wait.

'Adah Sharma? Are you Adah Sharma?' asked someone.

'Yes.'

'Please come with me and sign your attendance.'

I followed the girl in long boots. Who wears long boots in summers? I thought to myself. Finishing the pending task, I headed towards the cafeteria. Not in the mood to eat anything heavy, I decided to buy bread omelette. Suhana joined me in another fifteen minutes. She had managed to arrange notes of previous years from those girls. She was proud. I wasn't, for I did not understand the logic behind planning ahead of time. I believed in crossing the bridge when I came to it. The first day of college had been quite normal. It wasn't as exciting as I expected it to be. And hence, I wished that the forthcoming days were better and brighter to help me sail through the 3-year course easily. I was happy.

12

Quelle Surprise

Tossing and turning in the bed the previous night, I stayed away from sleep. Come dawn, my eyes refused to stay open. After spending the whole night playing Candy Crush, my eyes looked heavier and extremely tired. But alas! Attendance! Reluctant to leave the bed, I forced myself to finish the morning ablutions. Before leaving my room, I stuffed three biscuits in my mouth unsure of whether there would be any time for breakfast.

'Are you up yet, Adah?' Suhana shouted from outside.

'I am ready. Coming!'

'Bad luck! The first class has been called off. The teacher is absent.' She broke into a hysteria.

'Why God, why?' I said out loud further giving another reason to Suhana to continue laughing.

We spent the next hour in my room watching random videos on YouTube and then went straight to the class. Breakfast was out of the question because of the time constraint.

'I am going to divide you all into groups of five students each. The due date for the skit is 45 days later. Kindly ensure that each member of the group puts in efforts or else the marks for group work will not be added in the final score,' insisted my Psychology teacher.

We had been assigned an annual assessment for the year. Our job was to prepare a skit explaining the three zones in which everyone generally works. Those zones were the comfort zone, the panic zone and the learning zone. Since mostly all the members of my group had dozed off during the lecture when the teacher had demonstrated these zones using analogy and other relevant examples, I was the only one who had a clear idea about these concepts. Psychology always fascinated me. I loved to read Skinner's and Piaget's work.

'Am I the only one who doesn't understand the ABCs of these zones?' puzzled Suhana.

'I don't think so. Other than Adah, none of us can make head or tail of it!' Malik chimed in.

'I agree. You all don't even listen in the class; then how can you expect yourselves to understand the concepts.' I griped.

Knowing fairly well that I had to do all the research work, I mentally geared up for the upcoming weeks. I would have to work extra hours to ensure that the script of the play was ready two weeks before the due date. But that was not me. I couldn't plan ahead. Whatever mental preparation was en route, was stopped by my discouraging mind and my wavering heart that longed to be in my room, alone!

Post lunch, I decided to stay back for a psychology lecture on Cognitive Dissonance, a topic that Suhana despised. She tried her level best to discourage me but her pleas were not attended. The best thing about our college was that it organized such informative workshops quite often and they didn't cost a penny. For the students of Journalism, this extra knowledge came in very handy and it also gave them exposure in terms of meeting new and famous people. For me, it was a platform to understand how the writing niche works and how essential it is to develop contacts.

As I took my seat in the second row waiting for the host to begin entertaining us with the factual data, I absorbed the ambience. There was an uncanny similarity in the audience that had come to attend the lecture. Most of them wore spectacles and had a nerdy look. And then while searching for something unknown, I spotted him in the far end of the hall. He was the same boy from the day before. Wearing a black T-shirt that had something scribbled on it (which I obviously couldn't read), he was busy cleaning his spectacles. Soon I figured out that he was alone and had come to attend the lecture. Something in me urged me to walk up to him and ask him for an explanation. He owed me one. But then girls don't make the first move, do they?

As the lecture progressed, the crowd started getting thinner. Some left from the back door because the topic didn't quite interest them, some were audacious enough to let everybody know that they were leaving while some stayed.

'I request the people at the back to come in front and fill in the gaps. You know it is a sort of disappointment for the speaker when there are gaps in the seating arrangement!' admitted the speaker.

Not even in my wildest imagination had I thought that the boy from yesterday would come and sit beside me in the second row.

'Hi again,' he said with a genial smile.

'Hello,' I stammered.

I couldn't help but notice his half-crooked smile and his folded collar.

'How come you are here? Are you interested in psychology?' I quizzed.

'Not really, but I came here looking for answers,' he explained.

'That sounds intense. Are you on a self-exploration journey?'

'Ha! Not that way. Answers to questions that were given as a part of the annual assessment.'

'Oh, that! Which course are you pursuing?'

'I am studying Journalism. What about you?'

'What? No! I am studying the same. How come I never saw you? Which year?'

'I am in the second year. What about you?'

'I am a fresher. By the way, you owe me an explanation.'

'Really, what for?'

'Really?'

'I am kidding. I remember. I stole your lines because I did not have anything up my sleeve at that very moment. It was like a bolt from the blue. I was forced by my friends to get over the stage and speak.'

'That doesn't justify your mistake. You could have done something else than reciting poetry.'

'Well, have you ever experienced a brain-freeze moment?'

'Not brain-freeze but mouth-freeze for sure.' I wanted to say.

'Just because moments back I had caught hold of your green notebook, I thought what better way to escape than say a few lines on stage and get away from all the embarrassment! I am sorry. I know I shouldn't have done that.'

'That's alright. Anyway, I was not going to share these lines with anyone.'

'Why? They're beautiful. You should let the people around you know how well you write.'

I just smiled at his suggestion. He was the first one who had read what I had written. Never had I ever shown my book to my parents nor my sister. I was always under the impression that they would mock my interest and this belief became stronger when they chided me for choosing Journalism as my career. Who had the audacity to let the cat out of the bag and tell them that I wanted to become a writer?

A quick snap of fingers broke my reverie.

'What happened? Are you alright?' he asked.

'Yes, I am fine. So, if not a writer, what do you want to become?' I inquired.

'I want to become a Journalist, isn't that obvious?'

'Yes, it is.'

Only if I could explain to everyone what I wanted to do and do it without any inhibitions!

'Would you mind telling me your name?' I asked.

'Oh sorry, I am Darsh Kohli. And you are Adah, aren't you?'

'How do you know my name?' I gasped.

'Remember the green notebook? It had your name on the first page,' he chuckled.

The lecture went on for another hour and I understood that Cognitive Dissonance is a state of disquiet you feel when you have two conflicting beliefs. While on one hand, I didn't want to disappoint my family at any cost, I had chosen a path in life which they didn't approve of. My mind seemed to be in cognitive dissonance. It was being torn apart in the battle between choosing the family or passion.

'Would you like to grab a cup of coffee in the evening?' He asked.

'I would love to but I am a hosteler. I have time constraints.' I cautioned.

'That's all right. I am a hosteler too. I meant a cup of coffee in the cafeteria. That wouldn't cause a problem, would it?'

I thought for a while. It didn't sound right. Was it a date? Of course not! My heart was simply playing games and coming in the way of sound decision-making.

'Yes, that should be fine. What time?'

'Around 5? By then I would have finished my Basketball practise as well.'

'What? You play Basketball?'

'Yes, why is it such a surprise?'

'I also play that sport. Let's meet at the court then.' I chortled.

'Sure! I have never seen you on the court though.' He doubted.

'Well, if you are doubting my skills, then you are highly mistaken. I go there to practice immediately after classes, around 3 o'clock.'

'Nice! So, let's meet at 5 on the court.'

'Sure.'

After the lecture concluded, I headed straight to my room. I needed an hour of sleep before I went for the practice. Hugging my pillow tight, I tried to put my eyes to rest and in no time my eyelids gave in.

A loud bang on my door woke me up from the deep slumber. I had overslept and Suhana was creating havoc outside my room thinking that I had died in my sleep.

'What's wrong with you? One cannot even sleep in peace now, can one?' I rasped.

'Hello madam, a boy is waiting outside the hostel. When he saw me, he asked me to call you as he didn't have your number.'

'Which boy?' I asked and ran back to the window to try peeping.

'Darsh! What is he doing here? What's the time, Suhana?'

'It's 6 in the evening. Why? What happened? Who is Darsh?' she shot an array of questions at me.

'The boy I met in the Psychology lecture,' I tried sounding convincing.

'What? It's just the second day of college and look who has been so lucky already!'

'We'll talk when I get back. I am going for practice. See you.'

'Practice? With him? Are you mad…' her voice faded behind the wooden door. An uncanny and unfamiliar emotion had taken its toll on my mind and my heart. I was happy. There was something about Darsh that made me accept his invitation for a cup of coffee.

'Hi, Adah!'

'Quelle surprise!' I sputtered.

'Hello to you too. What does that mean?'

'It's French for 'What a surprise!',' I explained.

'You're late. Do you want to skip the practice today and head straight to the cafeteria?'

'I don't mind but then you could have told me before and I wouldn't have wasted time putting on the sports gear.'

'If I could have, I would have.'

'Are you a fan of Patrick Dorgan?'

'Yes, how do you know? Now, don't tell me that you listen to him too.'

'No, I don't. My father listens to him a lot.'

We headed to the cafeteria in our sports gear. There was nothing extraordinary about this meeting. But one thing that stuck with me was the freedom I got to be myself. Darsh seemed quite open-minded, he listened to all that I had to say without being judgemental. In return, I got to know how he was inclined towards media and journalism. He was smart and intelligent. The only thing he lacked was a blotch on his near-perfect life. His family was supportive of his career choice and that made a lot of difference.

We continued meeting more often after our first coffee rendezvous. He didn't have many friends nor did I. Basketball formed a common link between us and it blew away all the cobwebs. Taller and stronger, he aced it when it came to shooting. Shorter but smarter, I aced it when it came to defence. Gradually, I learnt the names of several other players from various departments. It was fun hanging out with them and playing. The one who suffered a great deal amidst all this was Suhana, for she had to wait for hours outside the court. Only if I had Viha with me there, the fun would have doubled. Still, I had Darsh now. He had become a good friend of mine over a span of 4 weeks.

13

Pleased as Punch

To love is to risk. Therefore, to love is to be brave. This quote is not by Rumi. I read it in a book. And it stayed with me. Why was I thinking about it, you may ask? Not because I was in love!

Darsh and I had been seeing each other quite often. We got along really well. Being my senior, he helped me with the question papers, which Suhana had already arranged but I still pretended that I needed them. It was a good topic of conversation. I helped Darsh overcome his stage fright by urging him to enrol in Talk-a thon, a platform for college students to overcome their stage fear by delivering weekly speeches. Suhana often said that we complemented each other but Darsh's friend thought otherwise. I couldn't understand why he disliked me. As days passed, I realized that my psychology project was due in a week. Assuming that I would have already scripted the play, my group mates also didn't remind me.

'I need help with the play,' I yelped.

'Which play?' Darsh asked.

'The play that our Psychology teacher had given as the annual assessment.'

'What's the topic?' He inquired.

'The three zones everybody should know about,' I explained.

'Oh, I know this one. The three very important zones- friend zone, enemy zone and the no-parking zone. That's easy!'

'Why are you suddenly behaving like you aren't the sharpest knife in the block?' I opined.

'Is this wrong? Then which zones were you talking about?'

'The comfort zone, panic zone and the learning zone,' I finished.

'Oh, of course. How could I not remember that!'

'Walking on air, aren't you? You didn't know a thing about this. Pretentious lad you are!'

'You think so?'

'Yes, I do. Now tell me what do I do with the script. Give me some ideas. Writing wouldn't be a problem. I just need ideas- that too by today.'

We sat there in the cafeteria thinking about all the possible real-life examples that could fit in the script. But failed miserably. Just when I had given up thinking and had decided to ask Suhana and Nidhi (another lazy member of my group) to come up with something, Darsh had his light-bulb moment.

'See Adah, your comfort zone is when you are with me talking about your inhibitions, your insecurities and your dreams and desires, right?'

'Yes, right. How is spending time with you related to this project?' I quizzed.

'Wait now. If you interrupt me, I might forget what I have to say.'

'Okay.'

'Now for you, stepping out of your comfort zone would mean that you would have to share the same things with a person who is not your friend but someone else. He can be your senior, your stalker or your lover, right?'

'You have gone insane. I have no idea what you are talking about!'

'Just tell me if this is right. Wouldn't you feel a little uncomfortable sharing the same details with such a person?'

'Yes, I would feel uncomfortable.'

'Well, that's your panic zone. You don't know what to do and therefore, you will become anxious and discouraged. You would think twice before letting your guard down. Does this make sense now?'

'It does, actually.'

'Now as we know that the Learning zone lies between your comfort zone and your panic zone, the perfect example of that would be if I propose you in another six months and not now. By then we would have established a better understanding and you wouldn't feel that discomfort. Does this make sense?'

'Yes, it does.'

'So, do you agree?' he chirped.

'Yes, I agree.' I nodded. No sooner had I nodded my head in affirmation than I realised what had just happened. Darsh had proposed. And in my utter dumbness, I had said yes!

'So, when do I meet your parents?'

'What? No, I didn't say yes to that. I didn't understand what you were trying to say.'

'So, is it a 'no' then?'

'No. I mean yes. Wait, why are you doing this?'

'Because I like you. And maybe, I even love you.'

Stupefied by what had just happened, I could not feel the ground beneath my feet. Had Darsh swept me off the ground? Or was it all a pleasant dream? I raised my hand to pinch myself on the cheek and that's when Darsh broke out into a roar of laughter. I thought he would say that he was joking. But he didn't say that. Instead, he held my hand and asked, 'Will you marry me once we finish college and are settled enough to begin a new life together?'

'Yes,' I mumbled.

Quite obviously we could not hug in public or else the very next moment we would have been expelled from college. But I was pleased as punch with all that was happening. I didn't plan on telling my family because they wouldn't understand. Upon asking Darsh if he was going to tell his family, he beamed with joy.

'Of course! I was thinking if you could come over to meet them this weekend?'

'Wouldn't they have a problem?' I asked.

'Not at all. I had already told them about you when I first developed a liking towards you. And guess what, my mother has been waiting ever since to meet you. You will enjoy the company of my people, I am sure.'

'But I am not sure if you will enjoy the company of my people,' I admitted.

'That's all right. You believe in crossing the bridge when we come to it, don't you? Then why to worry now. We have another two-three years before getting married. Or are you dreaming of it already?'

'Shut up!'

The next weekend I spent a lovely afternoon at Darsh's house. His elder brother and his wife were the nicest of all. They treated me like their own. Darsh's mother was comfortable looking 60. His father was confined to a wheelchair owing to an unfortunate accident that had left him paralysed waist-down. But that didn't seem to dampen his spirits even a bit. His dog, Kookie, was a sweetheart. She mingled well with the people her people loved. And that's the reason she couldn't stop licking my face. Darsh's niece was too adorable. Binging on the delectable snacks that his sister-in-law had prepared, I revelled with the new people.

'So, Adah, will your parents also agree to your marriage with Darsh?' asked Darsh's mother.

'Aunty, to be honest, I don't know. My family and I do not see eye to eye with each other. There are a couple of other beans that need to be spilt before them first.'

'Other beans? What do you mean?' Mrs Kohli (Darsh's mother) sounded perplexed.

'Oh, ma! She is a writer. You have to get used to new words like this. Beans mean several other things. Am I right, Ady?' cheered Darsh.

'Yes, of course. Other things like my career. My parents will not agree with my decision of becoming a writer. And revealing about Darsh will be like adding fuel to fire!' I fretted.

'Oh, don't worry dear. We will help you figure that out when the time is right.' Mr Kohli (Darsh's father) consoled.

'Let's all watch a movie together,' suggested Darsh.

'No, Darsh. I have to be back now. Suhana doesn't even have a clue where I am. If she finds out, she will panic and tell my mother. All hell will break loose!'

'That's alright. Ma, we will leave now. Can you pack something for dinner?'

'I already have.' Mrs Kohli declared.

She was such a sweetheart. She had packed a box for me as well. I wouldn't deny that I disliked the taste of the potato fry that she had prepared, but I respected the gesture. Without any hesitation, I took the box from my prospective mother-in-law and headed back to the campus with Darsh.

His house was in Rohini- quite far from the campus and that made me vexed, for I had to sit alert in the autorickshaw, covering my face as if I hailed from Taliban and was planning an attack on the Parliament. Darsh laughed at my precarious nature even though he was more fearful than I was. What made the difference for him was the fact that his family stood by him in whatever he did. This made him confident in his decisions. I was the opposite. I was dauntless when it came to public speaking or confronting new people. But I was a scared little mouse when it came to making decisions. All thanks to my family!

After meeting Darsh's family, my mind was at peace.

'How come you sound so calm?' asked my sister after a few days when I went home.

'I am always calm,' I replied sounding confident.

'As calm as a quiet sea, isn't it?'

'Why are you being a gobermouch?' I griped.

'Now what's that?'

'Figure out! The Internet is your second home. Why don't you knock at its door rather than being a gnashnab?' I snorted.

'There is no use of talking to you. You use wordplay and that is not fair,' responded my sister and hung up.

Aadrika, my sister, is like that. She cannot take it a bit if anyone hurled insults at her. However, she would never let her spirits dampen even if the person before her began sobbing. My mother didn't speak to me that day as she already assumed that we would end up fighting. My father did speak to me about marriage after college. I deftly diverted the topic towards my pending presentation and escaped further mental torture. That was indeed true. I needed time for the script. I had only four days in hand. Thus, like a diligent student, I sat down at my study table and started scribbling on the sheets. Darsh's analogy had given me an idea and I had found a raft in the ocean to hold on to.

14

A Close Shave

Osho says that if you love a person, love that person as a whole and not half. Love that person with all the defects because all those defects belong to that person and those flaws decide what he becomes. If you make an effort to change the person you love, it will imply that half of that person isn't loved. And that, my dear, is not love! In my case, Darsh was not the one with defects. I was the one with a lot of baggage.

'I have not come across any person who has had an easy past,' said Darsh, moving a little closer to me.

'That doesn't pacify me,' I argued moving away.

'Why are you so upset? We will think about all this when we have to deal with it. Why are you overthinking?'

'I am not perturbed by what you are thinking. There is something else.'

'Aren't you thinking about our marriage?' he asked.

'No, I am thinking about the THWR.'

'Now, what is that?' he looked baffled.

'The Himalayan Writing Retreat. It is one of the largest writing events that is organized in May. That is the time when we will have our exams. I have tried talking to the professors but there is only one way I can be a part of this event- by asking my parents to send a fax saying that I will be requiring a medical leave. Do you think my parents would ever agree to sign that application?' I finished. My heart sank at the mere thought of it.

'What are the dates for this event?' Darsh asked, looking at the calendar on his phone.

'They haven't announced yet. They have asked all the participants to send their confirmation in ten days. Also, this is going to cost a bomb. They are charging 15 thousand rupees for the entire trip. How will I arrange that much money?'

'Our exams will begin on the 15th of May, which is a Wednesday. I am quite sure that the organizers would have planned to leave either on Friday night or Saturday morning. Considering my guess to be correct, you will be able to attempt two papers at least.'

'You didn't even ask me why it is important for me to go there and not write the exams. How can you trust me so much?' I marvelled.

'I know how important it is for you to go to a writing retreat. It seems to be the only way possible to unleash your potential and explore the gift that you have. But I cannot deny that I will miss you. For how long will you be gone?'

'Five days. That will happen only when my parents agree. I don't know how to talk to them about this.'

'Leave all that. There is still time, isn't there? Come, let us check if your skit is ready. How are Nidhi and Suhana putting up? Is their cold war still on?' Darsh tried to divert the conversation but he failed miserably, for he didn't know that when I set my mind on something, even the worst of news could not take that thought out of my mind. I was stubborn and couldn't be pacified easily. Being bold came naturally to me but being bold at the cost of losing my family was out of the question.

'Try harder, Darsh. It is not working. Nidhi and Suhana are very much on talking terms.'

'Okay, okay! Come, let's eat something. Do you want to go to Chandni Chowk to have something nice?' he offered.

'Yes, I need to eat better if not feel better! What about the classes post-lunch?'

'I have Media Laws for two consecutive hours. I think I can skip that. What about you?'

'I have Media Management. I don't think I can skip that. But even if I attend, I will not be able to concentrate. I think we both have another Psychology workshop between 3:30 and 4:30. Will you attend that?'

'Of course, I will. Come let's hurry then.'

We headed straight to the Chandni Chowk. The smell of the melting butter, fattening oil and the never-ending sound of people talking filled our senses. It felt good to be a part of the chaos, for no one then could judge you or hear you or see you. But I was wrong.

A sudden unaccustomed feeling in my stomach made me flinch. Consequently, I dropped the curry on Darsh. I instantly asked for a tissue paper and started wiping the mess myself unaware of the mess that it would land me in. Just then, a cold hand held my arm. I shuddered to turn. But I had to. It was Aadrika. The look of disbelief on her face was a sight of rarity. While she gazed at Darsh who had stopped dead in his tracks, I looked over her shoulder to find my mother and my father hurrying towards us. My situation had dropped a bombshell on my family.

'What are you doing, Adah? Doesn't this boy have his own hands to wipe his shirt?' rebuked my father.

'I am just trying to help.' I quavered.

'It doesn't look like you are helping. It looks like you are mollycoddling your friend. Isn't he your friend, Adah?' snapped my sister.

Even though she was just two years younger, she never really empathized or sympathized with me. Allow her to put me into trouble, she will embrace it with open arms. That's what she did then- adding fuel to fire.

'What is all this, Adah? Don't you have a class now? Now I know where all our money is going. You miss your classes, come to Chandni Chowk to splurge on these street delicacies and then rebel in the house saying that we don't pay heed to what you want.'

'I am not splurging money, ma. I came here…' I was cut short by Nidhi who appeared before us like an angel in disguise.

'…to buy the costumes for the skit. Hello uncle, hello aunty. How come you all are here?' she chirped.

'Which costumes? What are you talking about?' queried my mother.

'Oh, aunty! Our psychology teacher had assigned us a play and we had to come and get our costumes. Hungry and tired that we were, we decided to stop by this shop and eat something.'

'Yes, ma. These all are in my group.'

'I know Nidhi and Suhana but I don't know this boy. He doesn't look of your age. He looks older.'

If ever there was an opening in a detective agency, I would have urged my mother to apply. Her prowess to get hold of the invisible evidence was commendable. Her gaze sent shivers down my spine. I knew that all hell would soon break loose. But then Suhana came to my rescue.

'Yes, aunty! You are right. He is not in our class. Nor he is part of the play. He is my brother's friend. He knows the shop owner and was here with us to get us the costumes at a cheaper price.'

'Adah, tell us honestly. If he is your senior, why were you wiping his shirt? He could have done it himself,' asked my father.

Caught in the whirlpool of questions, I was almost on the verge of giving up. My family was not credulous. They wouldn't believe a word that Nidhi had said. My mother especially was far from being Panglossian. She wasn't unreasonably optimistic enough to believe that my action was a mere coincidence!

'What? Why were you wiping Darsh's shirt, Adah?' giggled Nidhi and then continued, 'What were you thinking? Did you think he would bully you or scream at you?'

I was at the loss of words. I didn't know whether this move was to salvage my love or to push me into the hellfire!

'Aunty, she is mad. Yesterday, Darsh's friends tried to scare us all saying that if we disrespect any senior, we will have a hard time in college. I think Adah took it way too seriously.

Just because she spilt something on his shirt, she thought cleaning it would get her out of this mess,' defended Nidhi.

I waited with bated breath for my parents to respond. They didn't and that is what bothered me even more.

'Aadrika, come let us go home now,' instructed my mother and turned away.

No one spoke anything. I embraced Nidhi into a cwtch. She reciprocated. Darsh stood there like a stock-still mannequin. Suhana had receded into a corner by then. I was left wondering how the conversation with my parents on the phone would go. However, Nidhi seemed confident that they had bought her concocted tale.

As the sun decided to leave us alone with the moon, my mind started replaying the close shave on repeat. Within minutes, my phone buzzed and Aadrika's name appeared on the screen.

'How is your script going? Have you prepared?' asked my mother.

'Why are you calling from Aadrika's phone, ma?' I asked.

'There seems to be some problem with the volume button of my phone. Your father is looking into it. So, I thought of speaking to you using your sister's phone.'

'Oh, okay. The script is ready, ma. We have another two days and we will have to rehearse it well.'

'Why don't you send it to us to read. Let us see how well you write,' she proposed.

'Really? Why not! I will send it right away.'

My mother did not bring up anything about Darsh. And I did not have any plan to walk on the most dreaded path either. I convinced myself that all was well and that my relationship with Darsh was still a secret.

15

The Prolonged Learning Curve

'Study me as much as you like, you will not know me, for I differ in a hundred ways from what you see me be. Put yourself behind my eyes and see me as I see myself, for I have chosen to dwell in a place you cannot see.' Darsh grinned from ear to ear as he finished reading Rumi's quote.

'It applies to me,' I admitted.

'Really? You mean to say that I do not know you well, isn't it?' he queried.

'Yes, you just know me on the outside. You might be aware of my favourite things. But still you do not know what makes me immensely happy and peaceful. You do not know that I am so short-tempered that I might just bring the whole house down.'

'That's fascinating. I have a proposal. Do you want to listen to it?'

'Proposal? Again?' I asked.

'Not the marriage one! In order to get to know each other, let's play a game. Let's write down things that either make us happy or sad on chits. Make sure that you do not mention which emotion is related to that thing. Let's make two jars- one labelled as Adah and the other as Darsh. We will then exchange the jars. You pick a chit from my jar each day and I will do the same. Whatever is written on the chit, we will do that for the other person and indulge in a first-hand experience of learning the true side of each other.'

'How do you do this?' I asked surprised at his creativity.

'What? Shall I repeat?'

'No, not this. I mean how do you think of such ideas?'

'I am a Piscean. I am supposed to be creatively brilliant!' He beamed.

'I don't even believe in sun signs leave alone anything else.'

'You will start believing once you read this book.' He reached out for his bag and fished out a thick blue coloured book. It looked glossy from the outside. As I flipped through the pages, I could see some illustrations in the form of geometrical shapes and animal shapes as well. It was Linda Goodman's Book of Sun Signs. Darsh urged me to give it a try. Since I had rebuffed his earlier idea, I had no other option than to nod in affirmation. I decided to spend my weekend reading this book.

'So, did you like it?' He asked, tapping his fingers non-stop on the table.

We were in the cafeteria having breakfast. There were another 30 minutes for the first class to begin.

'Pisceans are quiet in the beginning but once you get to know them, they are a riot. Is that correct?' I enquired.

'That's for you to find out. How can I blow my own trumpet!'

'Well, I will eventually find out. What you need to know now is that we, Taureans, are emotionally very guarded...'

'And that is why you will always try to avoid unnecessary pain, even a heartbreak!' He completed without even blinking.

'Have you read about my sign as well?'

'Of course!'

I knew I had to be happy with the kind of response I got. But I wasn't. I felt a little scared- scared of letting all my guards down and exposing my vulnerable side. It had only been a few months, eight precisely, that we had known each other. But still there seemed an unfathomable abyss between us. There was so much I didn't know about him. He just seemed so perfect. And that was something my mind refused to accept. How can someone be without any flaw? I often wondered yet didn't get any answer. Sometimes, I felt like an onion- being peeled layer by layer only to be left bare and defenceless!

I had so much buried inside my heart that it seemed almost impossible to get rid of the baggage. Darsh, on the contrary, found it very easy to speak his mind and clear things at the spur of the moment. He believed in nipping the matter in the bud. The thought of not getting along later in life always worried me but he would calm me down by saying that if two similar people vowed to remain together for the rest of their life, the spice of life would be compromised. I would end up laughing but then soon realize that it did make sense.

After the mediocre success of the play, our group had become busy in completing other assessments and complying with the deadlines. Finally, when the workload seemed to take a toll on all of us, we decided to take a break from the mundane routine of classes by going for a movie on the weekend. While Nidhi and Suhana were vouching for Shah Rukh Khan's movie, I voted for Akshay Kumar's and the boys voted for none. They were not interested in any movie. Reaching a conclusion seemed impossible and thus, we all ended up watching The Village starring Bryce Dallas Howard and Joaquin Phoenix. It was awful.

'Did you like the movie?' I asked Darsh seating myself on the uncomfortable chair in our cafeteria.

'Yes, it was amazing. Did you see Bryce Dallas? He fitted in the role so well. I liked how this story was quite different from the usual thrillers. It had a mix of horror, comedy and action. What about you? From your expression, I am pretty sure you didn't like it!' He tried to challenge.

'No. It was rubbish. I don't understand the idea of making movies just to earn money. This one had such a predictable plot and the ending…what was that? How laughably stupid it was! Can you believe that no one, possibly no one, required medicine from outside before now?' I bubbled.

My tone was clear and it made Darsh realize that it would be futile to carry on the discussion. He decided not to respond and began checking his phone. I felt bad. A pang of guilt hit me hard.

'Alright, it wasn't so bad. Do you want to eat something? I asked changing the topic abruptly.

'No, you are not going to digress from the subject. You have to learn to become involved in a discussion even when you know that your view is different. Tell me, why didn't you like it?'

'Come on, I am not shying away from any discussion. I am not in the mood.'

Surprisingly, he didn't pester me further. We finished our tea and headed back to our respective hostels. We didn't meet up for dinner because I was, for some unknown reason, in a black mood. He did not force me to talk and assumed that it was better if I was left alone. He did say one thing before hanging up.

'Adah, think about it. If the conversation about the movie is bothering you, then we can talk. It is only me. I am not going to judge you. You can talk to your heart's content when you are with me. Try it out. At least once!'

That night I tossed and turned in my bed. What Darsh had said was right. Just because I couldn't express what I felt in entirety, the feeling of hollowness in my gut consumed my peace of mind. I had to get it out. And thus, I began typing a long message.

The movie was awful. I didn't understand the purpose of having a community in the first place if the people had not reached out to the outer world for medicines for decades. It was illogical. The ending, too, left the door opened ajar! People raved about this movie but I couldn't appreciate the idea of dressing up villagers in costumes to prevent the harm. That's why I disliked it so much.

I pressed the send button and went to sleep. I felt good.

The loud buzz of my phone hurt the interiors of my ears right in the morning. I had forgotten to put my phone on silent and consequently, when Darsh called, the ringtone deafened me.

'You are breviloquent! Did you have a good night's sleep?' He chirped.

'Yes, I did. You were right. I need to be more confident in voicing out what I feel.' I admitted.

'Why don't you try this therapy with your parents as well?'

The mere thought of it made my blood run cold. Explaining to my mother why I chose what I chose will be like fighting against a concrete wall. She wouldn't budge. But Darsh insisted that I speak with her, for there was a possibility that she might understand my point of view and then accept me as I am.

'Ma, I want to talk to you.'

'Is it about that boy in Chandni Chowk?'

'No, why would it be about him?'

'Because I know that something is not right between you two.'

I mentally prayed that my mother cut me some slack at least at that moment because I was trying to do something that I had never really thought I would do.

'I want to tell you why I took Journalism…'

'We know all about your whims and notions. It is now new to us. Why bring up this topic again when we have adjusted to whatever you wanted!' My mother spoke without any emotion. She was cold. And I feared what lay ahead if I began the conversation. I gave up. I did not have the guts to face her wrath and sardonic comments that would eventually make me question my own choices.

The next day when Darsh asked me about the entire fiasco, I had nothing to say. He understood and did not badger me further. The psychology class was scheduled in another 15 minutes and we all had to be there for our final scores of the play. Darsh also had his Basketball selections, so he went straight to the court.

'Students, it gives me immense pleasure to announce that Nidhi's group's presentation was the best and they have been given extra marks owing to the poetry recital that enhanced the overall impact of the play. Nidhi, you did a very good job of preparing this play and working in a collaborative atmosphere with the group.' My teacher showered all his praises on Nidhi who was not only indolent but also addicted to a life of pleasure. Something within me stirred and made me raise my hand. I shivered at the thought of the consequences but the damage had already been done.

'Yes, Adah, do you want to say something?' asked my teacher.

'Yes, Mr Das, I wanted to point out that it was not only Nidhi who did the work but all of us in her group who put together this great show. I think it would really lift our spirits if you acknowledged the efforts of all the team members.'

Mr Das was not like other teachers. He did not get offended by what I said. Instead, Nidhi's gasket was blown and she exited the class stomping her foot so loudly on the ground that for once we all felt that a natural calamity would put an end to our life at that very moment.

'What's wrong with you?' Asked Punit, who was another member of the group. A silent and shy Punit now knew how to raise his voice and ask me what was wrong!

'There is nothing wrong with her. She said what we all should have said. It wasn't right of Mr Das to give all credits to Nidhi, who didn't even move a leaf for this project.' Suhana came to my rescue.

Later that day, I tried hard to persuade Nidhi but she didn't seem in any mood of making up. When Suhana shared this episode with Darsh, his exhilaration knew no bounds. Like a happy camper, he bought a soft drink for me and promised to buy me lunch the next day. He was happy that I had stood my ground. I was happy too.

'Standing alone doesn't mean that you are alone. It simply means that you are strong enough to handle things by yourself.' He said when I admitted that I was happy.

That weekend I tried explaining to my parents why I opted for Journalism and also that I wasn't intending to become a journalist. I brought up the topic of Himalayan Writing Retreat. At first, my father was shocked and my mother was rendered speechless at my audacity to enrol in that program without even consulting them. But then Aadrika stepped in and for once, she behaved like my sister. It wasn't easy for me to convey to them that I wanted to become a writer. They had plenty of notions- how would I earn, how would I pay my bills, who would marry me, what would happen if I begin writing about my family and so on. I had no answer for all those questions, for the bridge seemed too far at that moment. I couldn't decide whether to cross it on foot or find an alternate path. As expected, my mother rejected the idea of going alone for the writing retreat.

'It is not even related to what you are pursuing,' she surmised.

The growing credibility gap left me in a quandary. I wasn't sure if my parents had understood what I had tried explaining. They were still stuck at the same point. It was as if nothing would change their opinion. Even Aadrika was shocked. She exchanged looks with me and then threw her hands in exasperation. But she didn't speak more and headed back to her room. My father found my mother's reasoning more convincing than mine. Hence, he refused to permit me to go for the retreat.

My broken heart could no longer pretend to be strong. I rushed back to my room, fell on the floor in a dishevelled heap and my sorrow poured out in a flood of uncontrollable tears. I did not eat nor did I sleep. Darsh kept trying my number, but I could gather the strength to talk to him and expose my vulnerability. I wasn't sad because I was denied permission to go, I was sad because I had failed miserably in making my parents understand what I wanted in life. It punctured my soul to live with the truth that the ones who brought me into this world were unhappy and dissatisfied by the choices I made in life. With all this happening, I could not even think of revealing anything about Darsh. It would be disastrous. This was a prolonged learning curve. I learnt that come what may, my parents will always misunderstand me.

16

As Fidgety as a Child

Two years later

The balmy rays of the sun peeped through the brown curtains afraid to look at the audience. The room was hot. The warmth was because of two reasons- one because of the presence of so many people in one room and the other because of the heated argument that had just begun. My family was agitated, I was in a quandary and Darsh stood before us all like an accused criminal who had managed to purloin the peace of mind that was there till the day before. Like an uncontrolled child, I had pestered Darsh to talk to my parents about 'us'. Turned out that they weren't very enthusiastic about the use of pronouns. Hence, my father repulsed at the thought of marrying me with Darsh.

'What on Earth is happening in this house? Has everyone lost their mind?' My father shrieked and stomped his foot.

'This girl will only bring us shame and nothing else. When we told her to do Engineering, she refused. Now, see the result of doing Journalism!' my mother did not shy away from making such a puny argument.

There are times in life when you feel so insignificant that the only thing that comes to your mind is to hide in some place and never be found. I had that moment then. My mother and father couldn't stop talking and rebuking Darsh. They didn't say a word to me because they deemed it futile to waste their words on me. Aadrika, as usual, had gone back to her room, least bothered about what was happening in the house.

'Sir, can you at least tell me why are you against Adah marrying me? I have already finished college and have an offer letter waiting on my desk. The package might not be great but it is a start.' Darsh tried to make the head and toe of the entire scenario by putting forth a valid point.

'It is not about your package. It is about what we will say to our friends and relatives who are under the impression that we will get Adah married to someone who can...' my mother's voice trailed off. It was quite evident that she could not speak her mind, for that would classify her as orthodox and stereotypical. Darsh belonged to a Punjabi family and we were Baniyas, not that any of that mattered to me. But it did to my parents. They were worried that I wouldn't be able to adjust to the new culture and that marrying someone of the same age will not help me in any way. Upon arguing that I will have someone who understands me better, my mother refuted that argument and said that it was all in my mind and would not be true when it would happen in real life.

Yet again I found myself at a juncture where I had no one to reach out to. It was up to me to either take a stand and go against my family once again or give in to their wishes and agree to marry a stranger. Knowing the likes of me, I was sure of one thing though- that I will not be able to adjust with a stranger.

It took me three months to finally gather courage, walk up to my parents and speak.

'Ma, I have decided to marry Darsh. I know you both will not agree but that's what I want to do. I will not marry him immediately after college. I want to work for a year and then I will get married.'

Strangely enough, my parents didn't say anything. When I asked my father to say something, he just said, 'We will cross the bridge when we come to it. There is no point of arguing at the moment and spoiling a Sunday for everybody.'

Another year of college finished and I was 22. It was too early to get married. Thus, both Darsh and I decided to focus on our career and then tie the knot. We hoped that by then my parents would also mellow down a bit and listen to us patiently. But life is not about how you plan things, it is more about how fate designs your path. Destiny rolled the dice and I got a six, at least metaphorically! My cousin, Lina, who lived in New York, had come down to Delhi for a month as she was visiting my aunt who lived in Paschim Vihar.

Since childhood, Lina and I got along really well even though she was four years elder to me. She was the chief editor in the New York Times and I adored her for her humility and helpful nature. Since she was an editor herself, she empathized with me. Thus, when she was in town, I grabbed the chance to hang out with her every day. She told me about how she was living her dream and how she had fallen in love with a boy in her office. It all seemed so fancy. But there was her share of hurdles as well. She missed her family and seldom got a chance to call them there because of the exorbitant airfare. She missed her friends and she was also boggled by the workload that kept her way too busy. Nevertheless, I only listened to the part where she said that she felt proud of herself when her name appeared in the newspaper every day. I wanted that for myself.

Lina had shared about an opening of a position for internship in NYT for that summer. I was overjoyed but soon grief took over my joy as I remembered how my chance to go to the Himalayan Writing Retreat had blown up in my face. My parents would allow me to get kidnapped but never allow me to apply for an internship outside the borders of our city, leave alone country.

'You have to understand, Masi. Adah is not a child anymore. You should not doubt her intentions, for they are as pure as the driven snow. She knows what she wants from life and that's why this opportunity is her best chance to get a job in a blue-chip company.'

'Lina, you don't have to speak on her behalf. She has been doing whatever she liked right from the very beginning. It is time for her to just work for a year and then get married to a nice young man.'

'Why a nice young man? What about Darsh? You know about him, isn't it?' Lina asked fearing the response.

'Yes, we do. But we did not say yes. I have started looking for a groom already. Mrs Sharma, my friend from the Satsang group, has promised to meet Adah after a month when her son will be home. He works in Dell and lives in Bangalore.'

'What? Does Adah know about it?'

'Of course, not! If she knew, all hell would break loose!'

Lina didn't argue the toss as she knew her words would make the matter worse. Brainstorming about how to get permission, I asked Darsh to help. At first, he seemed a bit hurt when I told him that my parents have started looking for a prospective groom but then he quickly brushed aside that thought, for he believed that would never be a success.

He knew that he was perfect for me. I knew that too. Intelligent that he was, he came up with a fool-proof plan of convincing my mother to agree for New York. In short, Lina had to convince her mother to speak to my mother about Pranit, Mrs Gupta's son, who worked in an MNC in New York. In other words, if I went to New York, I would be able to meet a 'nice young man' and forget Darsh. The plan would last for a year and then my parents would happily get me married to Pranit.

'What if Pranit doesn't reject me?' I asked, perplexed.

'Overconfident, aren't you?' mocked Darsh.

'No, seriously. It is a risk. I am very doubtful about this plan.'

'He would definitely reject you, sweetie!' Lina assured me.

'How are you so sure?'

'He has a girlfriend who works with me. They both have been living together for two months. Pranit wouldn't dare to tell his parents about her because they wouldn't agree. Hence, this is your chance to fly to America!'

I couldn't believe that God could be so kind to me. When Lina's mother spoke to my mother, the latter didn't budge. It took three days of continuous badgering and concoction of a zillion scenarios that would lead to blotting of my own copybook to get the nod. My mother realized that sending me off to America was a better plan than allowing me to stay in Delhi (in contact with Darsh). I, on the other hand, didn't mind the distance, for even Darsh had enrolled in a Master's programme in Mumbai. That was the most beautiful thing about our relationship. We both were not like those bouncy and giggly young lovers. We were pragmatic and supported each other in what we did.

Three months later

'When is your last exam?' Lina asked me over Skype.

'25th May. Why do you ask?'

'The internship will begin on 5th June. You need to ask Masi to book your tickets for 28th as it will take time for you to settle in my apartment and prepare for your first day. If we have some time to spare, I can show you around as well.' Lina suggested.

'Okay. I will try telling her that. She might give you a call to confirm. Please handle then.'

My mother readily agreed to talk to my father about the tickets and my dream of working for the NYT seemed plausible! Meanwhile, I studied hard and scored well in my final exams. Darsh had rejected the job proposal and had joined Xavier's College in Mumbai. Finding time to talk to each other in between our busy schedules seemed difficult, but we managed to speak to each other at least thrice a day. He would come to Delhi once in every two months and that is when I would meet him.

Another three months passed in a jiffy. With a lot of work on the plate and no time to think about anything else, the conversation with my parents was limited to general greetings, whereabouts and gossip sessions about our relatives and neighbours. I did not have much to say because they never took an interest in what was happening in my life. Hence, it was easier to cope when I didn't share much.

Soon enough it was time for me to prepare for a new venture in life. I couldn't help but be anxious and excited at the same time. Days were happier as my mother and my sister helped me shop. Their concern was genuine and I felt at home. My father, too, made sure that my documents were all set and that I had access to money when in the new country. He would talk to his friends who would then ask their children settled in New York about the lifestyle there and then my father would counsel me for an hour or so. It felt nice.

As the date for my departure neared, my stomach began fluttering with anticipation. On the D-day, my farewell turned out to be a little too overwhelming because my father hugged me and spoke using several unspoken words. Nevertheless, the joy of living my dream overcame the sorrow of leaving behind my loved ones. It was time to carve a path for myself. It was time to burn the midnight oil and proof to everyone that my choice of career wasn't wrong after all!

Have you ever pushed a cart filled with fruits down a slope? Can you imagine the trail it would have to cross? All muddy and bumpy- along with the fear of falling face down at any moment! I felt like that cart. I had been as fidgety as a child to make things happen in my life and when they began happening, I was scared- scared to go abroad, scared to work in NYT, scared to leave my family behind, leave Darsh behind and scared to come back. The ride would be bumpy and I knew it fairly well. Still, jumping the bandwagon was one of my favourite pastimes!

17

The Dubious Decision

New York

The fireplace was my tiny sun for the evening. The February cold was taking a toll on my health but the steamy hot soup that Lina had prepared was just the right food my body needed. As the fireplace cast shadows on the rug, I could not help but notice the crisp pop of the dry logs of wood that would soon be turned into ash. Even though the heat was only from one direction, it felt like the most needed thing for survival. Last few days had not been great. I had been under the weather and was unfortunate enough to be denied permission to stay home and rest. Thus, I had to go to the office and work on the pending article which required a survey of at least 50 people. The topic was one of my favourites- Relationships. My project lead, Judith, was working on this and I, as an intern, was expected to help her gather information from as many sources as possible. Lina had introduced me to some of her friends in the neighbourhood and I had made some new friends of my own. These were the only people I could ask questions about their relationship (s). Hence, the fieldwork was immense but my body was refusing to comply.

'No sane person would shy away from a taradiddle lie at such a point,' rebuked Lina.

'Judith wouldn't agree. She wants to complete this project as soon as possible. She might as well give me a pink slip than give me an off,' I said sadly.

'You have to try. It is worth a shot. Look at yourself; you look miserable!'

'No, I will manage. I just want this runny nose to stop being a tap!'

I knew deep in my mind that I would not be able to manage. Thus, after much badgering from Lina, I decided to call up Judith. Surprisingly, she agreed and it was only later that I got to know that she was tied up at her children's school and that's why she had given me a day off. Such are the rules of the world!

'Didn't you go to the office today?' Darsh sounded surprised.

'No, I am unwell. I just wish to get well soon. I am unable to enjoy the winter,' I growled.

'What? Unwell? And who was going to tell me that? Put Lina on call,' he commanded.

'What? No. There is no need to treat me like a child. Lina is not at home. She left for work half an hour ago.'

'You keep quiet. You need to be warm. Are you under the blanket?'

'No, but I am near the fireplace.'

'That's even better. What do you plan on doing today?'

'I don't know. I am quite bored actually. Can you suggest something?'

'I had something in mind already. Do you remember telling me about your wish to start a blog and write about your observations?'

'Yes, I do. That was in college- a long, long time ago!'

'Well, it is better to be late than never! Why don't you start that?

'I am not sure; I will have no time from tomorrow again!'

'Why do you have to think about that? You begin and we will see the rest. Don't back out without even trying.'

'But what if I am not able to continue that?' I asked sounding diffident.

'Do you know what my grandmother always said to me? She said don't ever say that you are sick. Say that you are healing because words manifest.'

'But I just called in sick…'

'Oh, come on, Adah! You know what I mean. If you say you cannot, it will never begin. Try at least.'

That was the thing about him. He had the prowess to come up with the right words at the right moment. I was the opposite. I was one of those people who would burst out laughing in dead silence over something that would have happened a year ago. His words did their task and that glittery dust of magic compelled me to begin writing. It hardly took any time to customize the blog settings. The real struggle was to write the first post. Like Lina had said earlier, people only follow those writers whose first few posts are engaging. Thus, making my first post 'engaging' took away more time than writing it.

And like that 'My Zen Spot' was born. It was a glimpse of my quietude and wise passivity. I posted my thoughts on things that mattered to me- my execrable social relationships, how I didn't get along with the usual normal, how my passion for writing was my Ikigai and a lot more about my life. At first, I struggled to keep up with regular posting schedule but Darsh did not give up on me. At least there was someone who trusted me enough.

A month later, I had gotten into the habit of writing something daily and could post three times a week. My blog was going well. People lauded my narration style and someone even forwarded the link of my blog to Judith. Well, she was kind enough to forward it to her friend who happened to be in the recruitment team. It would not take rocket science to figure out what came next. I was offered the job of Assistant Editor (Weekend Section) in the New York Times.

Excitement coursed like fever; my joy knew no bounds. I had done it. I had landed my dream job in my kitty. With brightened spirit, I dialled Darsh's number and gave him this exciting news. He was happy for me. Next, I called my mother but then realizing what would follow, I cut the call. My mind was in a mare's nest. I sat on the cushioned sofa and stared at the blank wall. If I were to take this job, I would have to work for at least a year so that my resume has something substantial. My parents would never agree to this. There was only one way I could convince them and that was to assure them that I would be paying my rent and earning enough to sponsor my ticket. Other than that, they would also need a slight hint of my liking towards Pranit. That was too much. Hence, I thought it was best to let Lina come back and think of something. Meanwhile, I also messaged Darsh to come up with a plan. I didn't want to miss this chance. It was a second chance, literally. The internship opportunity being the first!

The silent night and the freezing cold were enough to steal my sleep. As I got up to fetch another blanket, my smallest toe hit the side of the table and I screamed in pain. To my horror, I found Lina rushing towards my room and eventually slipping and hurting her foot. Swollen and red, my smallest toe stared at me, guilty. At that very moment, I realized two very obvious things- one, even the smallest of things can start a series of problems and have an entirely unexpected outcome; second, Darsh could become the little toe. I had my light bulb moment and forced Lina to hear it out.

'If Darsh meets papa by coincidence, he can initiate the conversation about his job and how he is looking forward to my homecoming. He can instil that restlessness in papa's mind.' I was too excited to notice that Lina had no clue about what I was blabbering.

'Hey,' I jerked her shoulder, 'wake up and listen.'

'I am listening but I am not able to understand anything.' She confessed like an innocent child.

I chided her and splashed some water on her face knowing fairly well that she would not leave any stone unturned in returning the favour when she was in her senses.

'What? What is wrong with you, Adah? It is 3 in the morning and you want me to listen to a story! Can't I sleep for some more time?'

'No, you cannot otherwise I will forget what I thought of!'

'Okay. Go on,' she agreed.

'So, I was thinking what if Darsh meets papa in the market by chance and then starts talking about his job and how he wishes to see me soon. My father will surely not be able to fathom this and will try to keep me away from Darsh by hook or by crook. Since Pranit is not interested in marriage, he will have no other option than to agree with my staying here and working in NYT. How does this sound?'

'Sounds fine to me but I still think that the result is not hundred per cent guaranteed!'

'That's okay. After all, I am playing with fire, aren't I?'

'Ha! Did you tell Darsh?'

'Heck no! He must be sleeping at this hour.'

'And what do you think I was doing?' She did sound angry.

'You were already here in my room, so I thought of grabbing the opportunity,' I admitted sheepishly and planted a kiss on her cheek. She mellowed down a bit and gestured me to leave her alone.

The next day, I explained everything to Darsh and he seemed fine with the plan. He decided to intentionally collide with my father on a Saturday when my father would be out for his morning walk. The fool-proof plan began on a good note as my father recognized Darsh when he pretended to bump into him but soon his attention wavered when I was brought up in the conversation.

'Why are you excited to meet my daughter? Are you still in touch with her?' asked my father.

'Of course, sir. I am really glad that she will be coming back soon. I am quite settled now and ready to begin a new phase of life. My parents are also eager to meet Adah.'

'What? Why do your parents want to meet her?'

'Have you forgotten already? I came to your house last year and I told you about how much I love your daughter and that I would like to marry her.'

'Oh, that! Yes, I remember. But I am not sure if Adah would still be interested. She has been seeing someone else,' explained my father.

'Is that 'someone' Pranit?' Darsh smirked.

'How do you know his name?'

'Sir, Adah and I are very serious about each other and thus, I know all about Pranit.'

The last line hit the bull's eye. Under the fardel of all those revelations, my father did what was expected. He called up Lina to ask if I was still in contact with Darsh and she did what I had told her to do.

'Mausaji, I think I have a solution. Adah has been offered a job here in the same company. If she takes that up, she can be here for some more time and can reconcile with Pranit. I will see to it that she does that.'

I mentally applauded Lina for her sheer brilliance in lying on the face. She was so guilt-free!

It took some time but my parents agreed and I gave my nod for the job. The dream was coming true. I had always fantasized about walking to my office that would be located in Times Square. This was it. I would think about buying a hot cup of coffee from the food trailer and greet everyone on the street. I had been doing that for some time now. The only things missing were the long coat and the coffee because they would look good on an editor and not on an intern!

'I am proud of you,' exclaimed Darsh.

'I know. Thank you for everything and I love you. I wish you were here with me to celebrate,' I chimed in.

'I know but cannot help being far. Anyway, I was thinking about what to do about getting married. Have you thought about it?' His question took me by surprise.

'No, I haven't. But now I am thinking. Won't it be difficult to convince my parents for our marriage?' I asked.

'It will be and that's why I am a little worried. One year will fly in a jiffy. You know how good time passes soon while the bad time lingers on forever.'

He was right. I had already started feeling like the trickster who always had tricks and plans always up her sleeve! I felt guilty and there was no way to get rid of that. Remorseful yet happy, I didn't know what destiny had in store for me. I was also scared, for my mother always said that if too many good things happen consecutively, brace yourself for impact as the joyride would soon come to a stop! Was it true? Well, I was going to find out soon. As for now, the dubious decision had been taken.

18

Making Headway

One year later

The warm Delhi air played a very bad host; it gave me the flu as a welcome gift. After having strained my back and my hips for more than a day, I was back to my roots. I was feeling great. The excitement to meet everyone and share personal stories was immense. My father had come to pick me up at the airport. He was elated to see me. The moment I hugged him, I could tell that he was overwhelmed and thus, couldn't say anything. A few minutes later, the taxi arrived. No sooner did we get into the cab than someone shouted my name. I turned back to look for the source but nothing was in sight.

'What happened? Did you forget anything inside the airport?' asked my father.

'No, no. I thought someone called my name.'

'Must be something else. There is so much noise here already. Come on, let's get in fast otherwise we will turn to ash.'

Yes, it was that hot in Delhi. The sweat was trickling down my cheek and I had no handkerchief to wipe it. Just when I rummaged through my purse to take out a tissue, someone grabbed my arm and twirled me in the opposite direction.

'What are you doing here?' I gasped.

'I am here to welcome you,' Darsh chimed in.

'What is he doing here?' shouted my father almost tripping over the suitcase that formed a weak border between Darsh and him.

'As I said, I am here to welcome Adah.'

Fuming with rage, my father played the Amrish Puri of DDLJ (Dilwale Dulhania Le Jayenge) and pushed me into the cab. Poor Darsh! He was no Shahrukh Khan to put up a tough fight before my father. For some strange reason, I burst out laughing once we hit the road.

'You come home after such a long time and you do not waste a second in embarrassing me. And then you laugh about it!' denounced my father.

'What did I do to embarrass you? It is not my fault that Darsh came to the airport.'

'Who told him about your arrival?'

'I did. But I did not ask him to come and meet me there. Do you really think, papa, that we would have stopped speaking to each other just because we were far away? Well, if you think that way, then you are wrong. I still want to marry Darsh and he does too.'

My father didn't respond. I knew that was the calm before the storm. My mother had been right. The joyride would get over one day and that day, I thought, was not far.

A week went by and nobody spoke anything about Darsh. Even when I tried to bring up his name, I was shushed with a wave. Then finally one day I decided to face the music. I caught hold of both my parents in the dining area and made sure that Aadrika was not at home.

'Ma, Pa, I need you to listen to me. I want to marry Darsh. Please understand that I love him dearly and I know that he is the right person for me.'

'Here begins the nonsense again! I am going out, Aarti. I need some air,' my father's sardonic remark hurt a lot. He wasn't even ready to confront me. How would I ever get him to agree, I wondered.

That day the conversation didn't happen. My father left the battlefield making me feel like a complete loser. It is said that the greatest gift you ever give someone is your time because when you give someone time, you give them a part of your life which will never come back. My parents never gave me time. Right from childhood, they pretended to not listen to what I had to say. For them, I was always wrong. They always claimed that what they were doing was for my good. Even if I agree to that, don't I have the right to express my desires and then be denied. They wouldn't lend an ear to anything that I had to say. They still did the same thing.

I caught hold of my parents again after two days during lunchtime and that time, I made sure to lock the door so that no one left the room. Yet again Aadrika wasn't at home. I told my father to patiently listen and then make a decision. But he preferred not to respond. A feeling in my gut said 'No' but a feeling in my heart said 'Yes'. I wondered what I would be if I didn't fight to find the courage to do what was right. There have been days when my breath was caught in my chest and I knew that fear was gaining on me. But that day was not such. I had to choose to be brave and not end up being a mere puppet of fear.

'Darsh earns well, there is no problem with his age as he is one year older, his family is nice and I wouldn't have to live with all of them after marriage because we will shift to Mumbai. I don't see what the problem is. If you were to find a groom for me, you would have looked into these many aspects, wouldn't you? So, where is the problem?'

The forehead skin wrinkled and the eyebrows narrowed. There was an uncustomed silence at the table, not the one of happy eating. Each word that escaped my mouth, fell like a heavy pebble on the table. The stiffness of their jaws and shoulders sent a chill down my spine. Even my stomach felt tight. Then, my father looked up at me- not in anger, but with a more determined resolve to end the matter for once and for all. He seemed ready to deliver a long monologue.

'His caste is a problem. We live in a society where there are certain rules and regulations that everyone has to follow. If you break those rules, society treats you like dirt. Your existence ceases and your self-respect is trodden over by everyone you know. I have worked hard my entire life and I will not sacrifice my hard work for your sake. You are young and your hot blood will not let you see things the way we see it.'

'But pa, discriminating based on caste is not legit, is it? Poonam Masi's son married a girl from another caste. I don't think Masi faces criticism of any sort. It has already been four years since he got married.'

'Oh yes? You are not aware of everything that goes on in the world, dear! Poonam's life has been horrible since the marriage of her son. She is unable to be a part of any social gathering anymore because when she is with other people, all they talk about is how she openly defied the rules of her community and let everyone down,' my mother put her oar in.

'Ma, it is not Darsh's fault to be born in a Punjabi family. I have known him for many years and I am sure that he is a good match for me. If you set me up with someone else, a stranger, will you guarantee peace and love for my entire future?'

'Love blossoms over the years after marriage. That's how your father and I fell in love- after we got married.'

'Those times were different. Two of my friends have filed for divorce because they are unhappy in their married life. When they agreed to marry a total stranger, they dreamt about moments of nuptial bliss but that was not in store for them and they didn't know that. You tried to set me up with Pranit. Do you even know what kind of man he is?'

'You never spoke to him then how do you know that he is bad?' asked my father.

'Yes, I never spoke to him but I know and I can prove that I am right. He has been living with his girlfriend for more than two years now. He doesn't plan on telling this to his parents as they are never going to agree. I know all this because his girlfriend works with Lina.'

The expression on my parents' face was horrifying but I couldn't help but enjoy that momentary victory.

'Imagine if I did a similar thing or lied to you about not meeting Darsh in America…'

'So, you did meet Darsh in America,' nagged my mother.

'I said "IMAGINE". Darsh was in Mumbai the whole time. You both can hire a detective and check. We didn't meet for two years. Even when I came to visit you all, he couldn't manage to come to Delhi because of a project. Hence, we didn't meet then as well. He is not taking any advantage of me. Can you please trust my instinct for this one time?'

Something had changed in them. I was sure. My mother constantly looked outside the window and my father cracked his knuckles.

'Would you both at least say something?'

'Okay. I think before we decide anything, we need to meet Darsh. When can he meet us? Is he in Delhi at the moment?' My father finished his line without even looking at me.

I knew it was hard for them but they had finally agreed with me on something. That was a good start or so I thought.

'Of course, he is here till the weekend. I can ask him to come tomorrow. Is tomorrow fine?'

'Yes, let him come tomorrow. Adah, I don't want you to be around when I am speaking with him. Okay?'

'Why? Are you going to hurt him? Or speak something nasty to him?'

'No, I will not do any such thing. Like I trusted your instinct, I need you to trust mine now.'

I nodded and prayed to God to be merciful towards Darsh.

'What? Really? They want to meet me! Should I bring my mother along?' Darsh sounded too excited that I had to warn him of the trouble that could shatter all his happiness.

'No, no. He wants to meet you alone and that's why I am a little scared. I have no idea what he would say to you. He has also asked me to be away when he is having a conversation with you.'

'Ahaa! Do you mean to say that he wants a man-to-man talk?' he smirked, a wide grin escaping the corners of his lips.

I so wished to kiss him at that very moment. But we were not the ones who could allow affection to become a public display of entertainment. We did not want to ruin the moment nor hurt our parents through our actions.

'Can you be serious at the moment?'

'Okay. I am sorry. So, what time should I come?'

'My father has said for 10 AM but you can come ten minutes early.'

'Don't worry, Adah. It will be fine. My heart says so.'

I wanted to believe his words but my apprehensions took control of my mind.

Waiting with bated breath, I marched up and down the pavement. What was taking Darsh so long to come? I wondered. We had decided to meet in a park in the evening. I wanted to know what my father had said to him.

'What happened? How did it go?' I entreated.

'Well, nothing great.'

'Why? What did he say?'

'He didn't say much. He asked about my job and where we would stay in case we got married. I told him that we would have to live in a rented apartment for a few years and then buy our own house. He also asked about my family members and whether they were okay with the marriage.'

'So, did he agree or not?'

'He didn't say that.'

'Then how did you both conclude your caucus?'

'He said that I didn't know how to convince the girl's father. Hence, I should send my parents to talk to your parents.'

I sulked. I didn't understand at first but then it struck me. Hope beaded my skin like dew on the spring grass. I felt like infusing that energy into my bloodstream to soothe my blood. I didn't know if my next day would be better than that day but all I knew was that I had won the first battle and that I was optimistic!

Two days later, Darsh's parents met with mine and all went well. Both the sides decided on the possibility of getting us married six months later and with that, they embraced two different cultures, two different beliefs and several different perspectives. Like a happy camper, I jumped around in my room. It felt like a prolonged war had come to an end and we, Darsh and I, had emerged victorious. We were ready to get married.

19 (a)

A Flicker of Hope

'Oh, so pretty! This would be a good choice for the Sangeet. What do you think?' Aadrika poked her head out from the tiny closet-kind area and gestured towards the green long skirt in her hand. Made from synthetic fibre, the skirt had deftly knitted multicoloured patterns on random places. In other spaces, the shiny golden stars embellished the vacancy.

'Does this come with a top as well?' I asked.

'Not really. But we can mix and match. What do you think about this yellow?'

Aadrika picked up another piece of clothing that was lined with embroidered borders and had small watermelons printed on it.

'I have to get married and not become a fruit-seller. Can you look for something more related to the occasion?'

After a very long time, I had seen my sister so enthused by something. She and I didn't see eye to eye. Hence, when this shopping schedule was decided, I convinced my mother to let me shop with my sister; I wanted to work on our bond. She had a remarkable taste in clothes. She was sassy at such a young age. Preparation for the semester exams had taken a toll on her and that's why she spent most of her time either in her room or with her friend, studying. There was no doubt in the fact that she was as cunning as a fox and could think on her feet. That was proved when she escaped the punishment every time her teacher called our mother for the Parent-Teacher Meeting.

'What about this red one? It is made from velvet-silk and has small golden stars on the borders. I think this will go well with the skirt.'

'Yes, wow! This is so beautiful! Now we only have to look for Dupatta.'

'What? That's all? Nothing else to shop?' She sounded tense.

'No, I meant that's all we have to look for in this shop. We shall then go to check out the matching footwear.'

She felt relieved because otherwise mother would have asked her to study. We meandered on the walkways of Canaught Place for another three hours or so and finished one round of shopping finally. Upon showing my outfits to my mother, her response left me struck dumb.

'What is wrong with you, Adah? What kind of weird colours have you picked? A green skirt and a red top? Really? You will look like a clown on your big day!'

'But ma, Aadrika picked these up and I liked them. They are trendy!'

'Don't blame your sister for this. I am sure you would have forced her to agree with you just like how you forced us to agree...' her voice trailed off. She went into the kitchen. I think it was intentional so that she would be excused from completing the statement. At that moment, I realized that

that decision of my life was not just a decision. It would have such a severe impact on my life that I might end up regretting it. I was quite aware of the fact that life could not be viewed through rose-tinted glasses and thus, I could anticipate what my parents would say if I ever came to them with any problem in my married life. In a nutshell, I was on my own- with no support system, nobody's shoulder to cry on and no one to become my interim agony aunt. That sent a chill down my spine. But the damage had been done. I could not back out. I would not back out because I wanted to marry Darsh. In him, I had found a partner who brought out the best in me. Then why should I let go?

I didn't respond to my mother's derisive remark. Walking back to my room with my clothes, I switched on the lights only to find a sealed envelope on the bed. It read: Dearest Wife-to-be. I rushed outside and asked my mother if Darsh had come home. Her ridicule didn't end with my clothes because what she said after my question made me vow to speak as less as possible with her.

'No, he didn't. Talk some sense to that boy. He is sending you letters now! What's wrong with him? He could have called- as if you both do not talk on the phone already. This drama is too much!'

Just when I was walking back to my room, I could hear Aadrika telling my mother, 'Ma, can you just let her be? You don't have to insult her at every point! What do you think you are doing?'

My mother, as expected, did not say anything in her defence. That kind of scene became a routine at my house.

I tried to divert my attention by reading Darsh's letter.

As the hues of the mist fall upon the foggy window,
I see your chimaera in all its glory.
My fingers trace the outline of your body,
My soul searching for our new story!

With every step that we take from now
You won't ever feel you're alone anyhow.
Like the street light on a lonely street
In times of darkness or glory, I wouldn't let you be unaccompanied.

In sorrow and in the joy that we will share,
I promise to be an extraordinaire;
But you promise me too to be with me
Because my life would be meaningless without thee!

The verse left me goggle-eyed. There were no tears, for I wasn't that sentimental. But Darsh had completed my verse. That was such a nice gesture! I didn't know what to do. Yet again the pangs of loneliness stung me. I wanted to share that with someone. But I had no one. Nidhi and Suhana were far away, quite literally. Nidhi was in Seattle pursuing her post-graduation while Suhana had gone on a solo trip to Bhutan. But I was not the one who could be broken that easily. Hence, I dialled a number.

'You are such a sweetheart!'

'Which means that you got my letter! Did you like it?'

'Of course, I did. I love you so much. Thank you for this. It is so special.'

'Then let's meet for dinner tonight?'

'Not really, my parents wouldn't allow.'

'Don't worry. You are not the only one being invited. I have invited your whole family. I shall pick you all up by 7. Sounds good?'

'Of course. That's perfect! I shall wait for you.'

I mulled over the way to tell my parents that they had been invited over for dinner by my in-laws. Soon, my sister came into my room and squeezed my cheek.

'Wow! Your would-be-husband is so cute! He has invited all of us for dinner,' she chirped.

'Really? How do you know?' I tried to pretend as if I knew nothing.

'He just spoke to pa. And don't worry, pa sounded okay with the plan. Just don't go and begin speaking to ma or pa showing them how excited you are. Let it go with the flow.'

Saying that she turned in haste to go back to her room. I held her arm and whispered a thank you. She understood my intention behind it. Aadrika was being nice to me and that meant a lot.

That evening was characterised by laughter, sarcasm, booze and desperate-to-leave guests. The facade of a happy family reunion was short-lived and thankfully, we all dispersed before the curtains came down. With only a month remaining for the wedding, my mother's spiritual side was awakened one fine day and she rummaged through the cupboards to find my 'Kundali'. Following that, she came running to me and asked me to tell Darsh that matching Kundali profiles was imperative before getting married.

'He doesn't believe in all this. He wouldn't even know if his Kundali was even made,' I admitted.

'As if one rebel wasn't enough that now we are inviting an atheist into our house!' She quipped and reminded me to just ask Darsh for it.

I tried convincing Darsh to hand over his Kundali to me the next morning and he didn't seem to like that idea. He didn't know where that paper was. I advised him to ask his parents but they didn't know either because they weren't too inclined towards the idea of believing the religious gurus. I had to tell my mother that bitter truth as fait accompli. She hurled some more remarks at Darsh even though he wasn't there to hear them but then she just stormed off. Despite that, she booked an appointment with the soothsayer (or so I would call him). Anxious to know what the soothsayer must have told my mother, I convinced Aadrika to find out. She agreed provided I let her get a picture clicked with Darsh so that she could show him to her friends.

'Ma went to that priest today and asked her to make a new Kundali for Darsh jijaji based on his date of birth and time of birth,' articulated Aadrika.

'How does she know the time of his birth?' I asked.

'She called him up to ask this morning.'

'What did the priest say?'

'She refused to make the Kundali. She first asked Ma if you two were having a love marriage or arranged marriage. Upon knowing that it is a love marriage, she advised Ma to stay away from Kundali and all. That could come in the way of the children's lives, that's what she told Ma.'

'Really? I didn't know that some priests could be so good too! Then what happened?'

'Then nothing. Ma came back home. I don't think she is planning to go unless someone messes with her mind again.'

'Thanks, Aadrika. I was so scared of all this. What if that priest found something wrong with our horoscopes?'

'Why are you thinking about stuff that has not happened. Don't be a fool! Instead of brooding over futile things, think about what you will wear for Mehendi ceremony. Don't go for the normal Salwar Kameez look. We will pick something trendy. Something in Lapis. That colour is your favourite and it enhances your beauty too!'

Aadrika was right. I was simply thinking about the odds that weren't there. I got up from the bed and went straight towards the dresser. Inside the last drawer lay a thick red folder.

'Yes, yes! This one, bring this sweetheart here. Come to mama, baby!' shouted Aadrika the moment she saw the folder.

As we flipped the pictures of the designer Lehengas that were neatly filed in that folder, my eyes spotted a lapis halter neck gown.

'This is it! I need to get this. Look for the store's number,' I urged.

'It's here, it's here.'

We dialled the number but the person on the other side said that they did not have that gown. Left with no other option, I decided to go to Chandni Chawk and buy the unstitched material from some shop and then hand it over to our family tailor. The dress that Aadrika chose was luckily available at the same store. Hence, we saved some time at least.

We spent another ten days shopping for our dresses and the remaining days in helping out our parents with the photographer, the caterer, the venue, the videographer and the invitations. A wedding was a tiresome affair; it involved a lot of intricate planning. Even though that might sound alluring at first, it is the most tedious task ever discovered. Unlike how they show in the movies, mine was not a fairy-tale wedding. It wasn't going to be an elaborate affair. Just two-three functions in a wedding hall and that was it. After all, I wasn't Cinderella nor were my parents my Godparents who would use a magic wand to grant all my wishes. Darsh wasn't a prince either! His family was also not very affluent but they all had a large heart. I didn't want jewels or money.

All I wanted was a happy and peaceful life ahead. I wanted my parents to come to grips with the fact that I could make my own decisions. I wanted to experience the joys of marriage with Darsh. I wanted life to settle so that I could begin the real struggle of becoming a writer. That's all. Was it too much to ask for?

19 (b)

A Flicker of Hope

The sweet aroma of cardamom and black pepper filled the air. My nostrils struggled to identify the dish but they didn't seem experienced enough to crack the puzzle. The cooks had settled at the back and had begun cooking delectable meals for the D day. It was my wedding day and frenzied that I already was, I decided to take a walking tour of the wedding hall and see if things were ready. Thankfully, the hall was just at the end of the road, hardly a kilometre from my house. I pulled along Aadrika and we both were knocked down with a feather when we saw the main seating area. The decoration made the hall look palatial. With curtain drapes lined by sequins of golden beads, the hall glimmered with a yellow light. A large window allowed the sunrays to take a sneak-peak but that window wouldn't be of much use as the wedding would happen in the night.

I could smell lavender. Some of the workers were still arranging the flowers. The false ceiling looked as fresh as new. The combination of light blue and light purple seemed so pleasant to the eyes. Lavender orchids further added to the beauty.

'Hey, come here. Look at the stage,' Aadrika pulled me by my arm towards the staging area.

The stage looked like a gateway to a utopian world where only flowers and ribbons greeted the people. The beribboned cushioned sofa was cream but inlaid with soft pink silk; flowers embroidered so delicately that it felt that they might have landed there in Spring and just sunk in, but I knew it must have taken them hundreds of hours to sow.

The curtains at the back were cream- old but still not faded, the kind of cream that was untouched by hands and devoid of dust. I couldn't believe that I would be married in another few hours. The hall was my selection and I was happy that it passed the muster.

Aadrika and I then went to check how the food preparation was going on. My father was already there giving clear instructions to the cook and the catering team.

'How come you girls are here?' he asked, his tone firm yet mellowed.

'We just came to check if all was fine,' I responded.

'Well, don't worry about anything. I am here taking care of everything. You both go home and see if your mother needs any help there. With so many guests in the house, she must be going bananas. Also, when will the two of you go to the parlour?'

'We will go in another two hours. Till then, we will go and help mother,' suggested Aadrika.

Leaving the hall knowing that I would be making a grand entry in some time caused an uncanny sensation in my stomach. I was nervous, yes. But I was excited too, for I could already picture Darsh standing on the stage and waiting for me. The idea of spending the rest of my life with him increased the adrenaline rush in my body. It was a new adventure that I was going to take up not knowing how well it would go. My gut promised me that it was the best decision of my life but that's what it said every time I took a difficult decision.

Come late evening and I was ready in a pastel green lehenga and a golden top.

'You have two dupattas. I would suggest that you take the golden one on top of your head so that it contrasts with your lehenga,' asserted my make-up artist.

I could see how good she was. Deftly hiding my blemishes and the birthmark on my chin, she made me look like a princess. I had to agree with what she suggested and hence, the golden piece of cloth was clipped onto my head using umpteen number of pins that were enough to build a house! The artificial eyelashes felt heavy on my eyes and the jewellery was also taking a toll. Imagine how it would be to wait for the entire function to go on till the first rays of the sun appeared and then spend another set of hours meeting and greeting strangers in a new house! I didn't know if I was ready for all that yet!

When I took a few steps towards the main hall, the fluttering in my stomach increased. The hallway buzzed with the excited tittle-tattle and the children ran between the tall vases as if running in a game of tag. Then I entered the big hall and loud applause spread across like a riot. My eyes searched for Darsh and there he was, dressed in a black suit, immaculate and crisp, looking at me with adoration. I wanted to capture that moment in my heart, lock it and bury it so deep that even if someone tried to steal it, they wouldn't be able to find it.

'Are you ready to take the plunge?' he asked winking at me.

'Are you?'

'Of course, I am. I have been waiting for this moment for such a long time now!'

His words were a balm to my soul.

'Yes, I am ready. Let's just get married fast.'

And like that, we became man and wife. It was overwhelming to remember how we first met by accident and then eventually, got into a relationship, how we survived two long years of long-distance and finally on that day, we tied the knot. We did have a few obstacles in our way to get married yet we emerged victorious. If we weren't the perfect example of 'soulmates' then who would be?

The next day was filled with tears for my family, for they were bidding me goodbye and happiness for Darsh's family, for they were welcoming a new member in their family. After the family rituals, Darsh and I were asked to get some rest. The next day was supposed to be hectic again as another set of rituals awaited us. Phew!

'So, now what's on the menu?' Darsh tried to sound funny.

'What?'

'Come on, this is one of the famous flirty lines. You are supposed to complete it,' he sounded annoyed.

'But what am I supposed to say? I don't read such articles in my free time.' I admitted.

'Me and you (Me-n- u), that is what you are supposed to say,' he flirted.

I demonstrated a forced smile and he knew instantly that he took a wrong path to woo me on the very first day after marriage.

'Are you tired?' I tried to break the ice and also realized that the comfort and ease with which we both could talk to each other were missing. They had to be brought back.

'Yes, too tired of smiling incessantly for countless hours. Want some music?'

'Sure. Lionel Richie?'

'I Call It Love!' He jumped with joy. That was our song. Like how every other couple had a song that they could relate to, we had that one.

Music soothed the anxious nerves to some extent. We changed into more comfortable clothing. It was still a little awkward. My sister-in-law had sent red wine for us. The alcohol did the trick and soon, we fell asleep though I was sure that my sister-in-law had hoped that it would help us in getting some action.

The next day, after the rituals were over, we were to leave for Kalpa in Himachal Pradesh for our honeymoon.

Kalpa

Surround by the apple orchards and snowy mountains, our little cottage was the best place to be in the freezing December winter. The coarse, unevenly sized, grey stones that made up the wall were too cold to be touched. The curling trail of smoke that came from the tiny chimney hinted towards the warmth that we would get once inside. The fragrance of the yellow lilies that bloomed just outside in a small garden filled our bedroom. It was the perfect setting. The fireplace overlooked a woollen rug sprawled across on the floor. The faint light of the bulbs lighted the small cabin just well.

We kept our luggage in the storeroom. The hesitation seemed a little less. Maybe because there were no 'others' with us. While I adjusted the curtain that had developed a wrinkle or so I thought, I felt the warmth of Darsh's hands on my waist. Suddenly, a very different feeling engulfed me. I knew at that very instant that I wouldn't have to spend another day in a room alone with only my soul to give me company. As I turned to face him, the endearing look in his eyes made me weak in the knees. He knew that if he kissed me on the neck, it would make me crumble in his arms. He did just that. As his lips traced the path to mine, all my thoughts were stopped in their tracks. My mind was numb. After all, in moments like those, the mind should mind its own business! His hand ran through my hair and his kisses became more urgent. In another instant, he pulled me closer to his musk-scented body and then it was just one wish, one desire. We knew what we wanted and it was only a matter of time before it happened.

The next few days in Kalpa were busy- we trekked our way up the solitary mountains, met a few locals and enjoyed the cosy nights cuddling and making love beside the fireplace. It was the best time of my life. All the moments spent with my husband erased all the sad memories that had occupied my mind for a long time.

Darsh was expected to join work in another three days and thus, after we returned to Delhi, we did not have much time to spend at Darsh's parents' house. We had to leave for Mumbai. Once in Mumbai, the real dose of responsibility was given to us. Setting the house single-handedly and making an attempt to become a capable wife, I tried to manage everything efficiently. While Darsh got a promotion in another six months, I completed one month in my new company- The Economic Times- as an assistant editor. The entries on my blog- My Zen Spot- became very frequent and that helped me get the fluency in writing articles on issues in the society. Darsh's never-ending love and care were enough to let time fly quickly.

Come next December, we completed one year of nuptial bliss. He surprised me by baking a cake at home. I, on the other hand, surprised him with his favourite book- The Alchemist and a poem that I composed just three days back for him. While I wanted him to read the poem in his mind, he decided against my wish and tried to weave words into the music. He had begun learning ukelele a few days back and what could be more fascinating than watching and listening to him.

The faded hues of the old curtain

Remind me of the time I spent with you.

They take me down the memory lane,

Washing away the thoughts that are blue!

The emerald-green bottle of wine

That stands alone on the mantelpiece

Invites me every day to pop the cork

And call you over to toe the line!

Love is what makes me glow

Even when shadows lurk behind me.

I know you will come and hold me close,

Your silent whispers in my ear will make me know.

That was the sign of a beautiful person; they saw beauty in everything. Darsh was a beautiful person. He was too real to be true. I was living the life of Riley with him. Our weekdays were busy but our weekends were solely dedicated to the things we loved. I would spend time writing while he would spend time reading books. He made me acquainted with the idea of destination addiction- a concept that said that destination addiction was a preoccupation with the idea that happiness is in the next place or next job or the next partner. Until you give up the idea that happiness is somewhere else, it will never be where you are. What's meant for you will come and stay with you. You will not have to fight or force or feel desperate about it. What's meant to fall apart, will fall apart and no one will be able to stop it. Instead of feeling unworthy and stressed, you should find your inner peace so that you can bring your best into each moment.

'Do you think it is easy to be satisfied and happy with whatever life offers us?' I would ask him often expecting him to change his point of view. But he was one stubborn man.

'Yes, it is true. You need to realize that happiness is not a hidden gem. It is an experience that cannot hide. It has to be found. There is joy in every moment. Only when you decide to let your heart experience and feel that joy, you will be satisfied and happy at the same time.'

I would never argue with him because I knew he held that belief quite close to his heart and I didn't want to burden him with me always being a doubting Thomas! It was only with time that I realized that his positive energy had changed me as well. My point of view had changed.

'You have changed. You have become more patient. You don't get bothered by Ma's remarks anymore,' Aadrika would often say.

But I always took her words lightly. Darsh had changed me for good. I was more confident in his presence and more vocal as well. He made me face my fears and that made me stronger, mentally. That one decision of marrying him and making him the most important part of my life was the best decision I could have ever made. Hence, I started believing that I knew my mind well and I knew what I wanted in life. At the same time, I also used to remember my mother's words about the joyride coming to an end. I hadn't faced a lot of troubles unlike how many people face. That scared me. Life seemed like a bed of roses. I didn't want the thorns to ruin my paradise and thus, the overthinker in me would be stimulated at every little opportunity. Darsh would try to calm my mind but it would bounce back again after some time. Only if I knew what was in store, I would have tried to make things better.

20 (a)

Twist in the Wind

The sitooterie was set up for a small afternoon party. My friends, Nidhi and Suhana, were in Mumbai for some work and they had decided to come over to my house and spend some time together. Darsh was in Pune for a meeting and was supposed to return by the next morning. Hence, I had the whole house to myself and could focus on making my friends' stay comfortable.

'Hey, you! Look at you, you haven't changed since we last met!' chirped Nidhi.

She had put on a little weight and that made her look so cute. Suhana was still the same. Her hair looked a little different though but those were only temporary highlights.

'So, what's up? How is life after marriage? When are you guys going to plan for a kid? It's what- four years already?' asked Suhana.

'Yes, we just completed four last December. I don't know. We don't want a child at this point. We are happy devoting time to each other. And it has been only four years…'

'Not two. You both have been together for such a long time. How many more years do you both want to know each other?' Nidhi cut me short and we all ended up laughing.

Darsh and I were clear about one thing- that we wouldn't have a child only because our parents wanted us to bear children. We would metamorphose into a responsible adult when we think we are ready and that solved half of the problems of our life because we didn't waste time fighting about this. Having a clear mindset and discussion with your partner often helped solve major problems. We did just that.

I had prepared a lot of snacks for those girls but they hardly ate anything. They left by 6 in the evening as they had a train to catch. Happy that I would have eatables to munch on, I took out the leftover whiskey and poured myself a neat peg. Plugging on the television, I searched for a thriller movie. Having found 'Kaun' playing on television, I made myself comfortable on the bean bag and braced myself for a solo night! That day I might have slept at around 4 AM. Darsh had left me a message that he had booked the cab and would leave from his hotel by 3:30 AM. I had tried my best to persuade him not to travel in the dark of the night but he wouldn't listen. He said that he had to be in his office by 7 in the morning and hence, it was imperative to leave early from Pune.

The whisky must have diligently done its job because I didn't remember when I fell asleep. However, the unabating ringing of the landline phone disturbed my sleep. With half-open eyes, I squinted to look at the clock. It was 6 in the morning. How come Darsh hasn't come home yet? I wondered and sprinted to answer the phone.

'Hello,' I spoke breathing with difficulty, my mouth emitting a disgusting smell that felt familiar.

'Am I speaking to Mrs Kohli? Mrs Adah Kohli?'

'Yes, I am Adah. Who is this?'

'I am calling from Gandhi Hospital, Panvel. Do you know Mr Darsh Kohli?'

The question sounded ambiguous. Why would someone call me by my name and then ask me if I knew my husband? Something was wrong and terrible.

'Yes, I am his wife. Why have you called me?' I asked trying to stay calm.

'Ma'am, please come to the Gandhi Hospital as soon as possible. Your husband has met with an accident. He is in a critical condition and is in the ICU.'

My brain stuttered for a moment and my eyes took in more light than expected. Every part of my body went on pause mode while my thoughts caught up. I dropped the receiver on the ground and fell flat on the ground. Every wisp of air had been snatched from my lungs and I found it difficult to exhale or inhale or do anything. Taking a whole two minutes to absorb what I had just heard, I heard the man, on the other hand, shouting my name so loud that it could be heard from the receiver.

'Yes, I am here. I will be there. Thanks for informing. Can you please be with my husband till I come?'

'Yes, of course. Don't worry madam, he will be fine. I am here with him. You come soon.'

I gathered all the courage I was left with. There was no use of sitting and lamenting and not doing anything. I called up my father and asked him to inform Darsh's family and ask his brother to come over to Panvel soon. I needed someone by my side. I changed into my pants and booked a cab to the hospital. On the way, I called Darsh's colleague, Rahul, too. He started from the office the very next minute and promised me to meet me at the hospital. The one and a half-hour cab ride took forever. My fingers danced rhythmically as if in a spasm. Gradually, the churning in my stomach intensified and I could not bear the horrible thoughts that clouded my sane judgement. I prayed and prayed for Darsh. I just wanted him to be fine.

At 7: 45 AM, I reached the hospital. The placed reeked of a smell that had nothing positive about it. A distant wail grabbed my attention and I couldn't help but think of something bad that had happened to Darsh. I reached the reception and asked the lady there about Darsh.

'I am Darsh's wife. He was admitted here this morning. He had met with an accident.'

The receptionist didn't say anything. Instead, she gestured me to follow her. Clueless and hapless, I paced across the hallway and finally reached a room that was dimly lit. Wondering why they had put Darsh in such a dimly-lit room, I asked the receptionist, 'Why are the lights so dim?'

'Hey, Adah. Where is he? Did you see him?' It was Rahul accompanied by Priya, his wife.

'He seems to be inside. See how dimly-lit this room is! How are they treating him in this?' I quavered.

Just then an unfamiliar face appeared from behind Rahul.

'I am the one who called you, Ms Adah. I am Kumar. Can I talk to you in private?'

I dreaded what he wanted to say. Why were they not allowing me to see Darsh? Kumar had said that Darsh was in the ICU but the receptionist brought me to that room. If Darsh was critical, why would they shift him in a room? All such questions flooded my mind and a cloud of doubt darkened.

'Mr. Darsh's cab collided with a mini truck that was trying to overtake from the other side. The collision was so severe that the steering wheel barged right into the cab driver's chest and Mr Darsh, who was in the passenger seat, suffered a severe impact on his head; it hit on the front glass. By the time I brought him to the hospital, he was no more. I urged the doctors to at least check and try reviving him. But all that failed. I had to lie to you on the phone so that you do not panic. The doctors told me to be careful with my words. I am so sorry for your loss. Please let me know if I can do anything to help you.'

I was as white as a chalk. My eyes and my mouth were frozen wide open in an expression of stunned surprise. My face was sunken and haunted. My mind was cold and empty. Priya helped me regain my balance. I couldn't fathom what Kumar had just said.

'I want to see him,' I announced.

'Would you like to wait for your family members to come? Their support is what you need at the moment,' advised Priya.

'No, I want to meet him alone.'

'Adah, he is no longer with us. You cannot meet him. You can just see him.' Priya tried to bring me back to reality. It was harsh.

A nurse came our way and held my arm gently, guiding me to the room in which my dead husband lay. I was fortified seeing a body wrapped in a white cloth that had patches of bloodstains. The sight made me feel that there was no oxygen in the world and that lack of oxygen descended on my mind, taking control of the other senses and knocking me unconscious. I must have been benumbed for more than four hours or so before I opened my eyes again. The pale of my skin sent shivers down my mother's spine. Yes, my family and Darsh's family were there. Amidst loud wailing and silent sobs, I could hear my heart crying and my gut trembling. I could feel my body shattering into a thousand pieces, each piece further crumbling into smaller pieces. The love of my life was gone leaving me alone.

Darsh's family couldn't be consoled. It was the first time I didn't see them smile. Their cries crippled my spirit. Seeing my father cry was another blow on my soul. Darsh's death had had a devastating effect.

After the funeral and other rituals were over, Darsh's parents asked me to move in with them. At first, I didn't respond. But then, soon I realized that I had to give them an answer. They were sailing in the same boat as me. They had lost their son and it was the most horrible thing that could happen to parents- watching their child pass away before their eyes. Death wasn't kind, I knew that. It snatched what it could when it could and whatever it could. It didn't matter whether you were near or far. When death decided to roll the dice, you couldn't do anything but just play along. In a second, Darsh was gone. I couldn't believe it. I didn't even get a chance to bid him a proper goodbye. We were supposed to meet in the morning, weren't we? Then why did God have to take him away like that?

'I would like to stay here for some more time, mummy,' I told Darsh's mother.

'But child, what would you do alone? You need support and if we are not there to support then shame on us!'

'It's not that, mummy. I just don't wish to part with his memories so soon. We spent four years here in this house. Every corner of this house has a story to tell. If I move back to Delhi, I would deprive my soul of whatever is left of Darsh. I can only hang on to the memories now, isn't it?'

She understood. That was the best thing about his family. They understood what Darsh and I wanted. His father even counselled me to resume work after a week so that I have a distraction and I did that. It was difficult, very difficult. Life alone was miserable. Even after a month, Darsh's memories would haunt me and I would break out in a cold sweat in the middle of the night. Since his death, I didn't sleep with lights off even for a single day. In the darkness, I could sense a misty veil surround me. It was like the dead white trees stretched out their bony branches for the dark sunless sky! It was terrifying.

Three months passed too soon. I got used to my lonely lifestyle. I had stopped meeting my friends or going out with them for lunch or dinner. I mostly kept to myself, spending weekdays in the office and weekends in my house, in pyjamas. I was a mess and I knew that. Finally, when Aadrika visited me after a while and witnessed my miserable state, she told it all to my parents.

'It's time for you to figure out certain things for yourself, Adah darling,' cautioned my mother.

'Figure out what?' I asked baffled at that question.

'You cannot keep on living alone here. You need to move back to Delhi. Whether or not you live with Darsh's parents, that's your choice. We wouldn't interfere with that.'

'Why should I move back to Delhi? I am fine here.' I asserted.

'Aadrika could see how fine you were doing without Darsh. You need to accept that he is not coming back. You need to become more social. Your friends, Nidhi and Suhana, are there in Delhi. You will feel better if they are around you.'

'No, Ma. I do not want to move. Please can you drop this topic? I am not in the mood to listen.' Saying that I put the receiver down unaware of the next step that my parents would take.

The following week, on a bright Sunday afternoon, while I was napping with Pizza sprawled across the bed, I heard a loud knock on the door. The momentary thought of Darsh being there was brushed aside by the heart-wrenching sight of his dead body wrapped in a white cloth. I managed to get up and was caught unawares by the guest. It was my mother.

'I have explained everything to your father about how he will manage food and other household chores while I spend some time with you here.'

'What? For how long will you be staying here, Ma?'

'Till you agree to come back to Delhi with me,' she smiled.

'Please, don't start that again. I am happy here.'

'Then prove it to me. Let me stay here and if I am convinced that you are fine, I will leave you alone.'

I didn't want to argue the toss. Deep within I wanted company and who would be better than my mother. I just feared her sardonic remarks. But she didn't toe that line.

'Don't you feel like going out with your office friends?' she asked one day while sipping her tea.

'Not really. I like keeping my professional and personal life separate.' I asserted.

'Really? Do you even have any personal life left? Adah, you are too young to waste your life in solitude. Please, listen to me this once. Move to Delhi with us. Or you can rent an apartment. But just move closer to us, please!' My mother beseeched me and somewhere I realized that she was right. Clinging onto Darsh's memories wouldn't do me any good. He was not coming back at any cost. Even he would have wanted me to be happy. After all, happiness had to be experienced and not searched for. I agreed to move to Delhi, unaware of the fact that a terrible irony awaited me. What was urging me to move closer to my family would eventually lead to the distance growing so much that the abyss would only increase with time.

20 (b)

Twist in the Wind

'Move this sofa by the wall,' I shouted at the man who kept dragging the sofa on the tiled floor. It had been six months without Darsh by my side. 'Lift it, you fool. You are going to blemish these fresh new tiles.'

'Keep it cool, Adah. I will talk to him,' said my brother-in-law.

I had shifted to Delhi two weeks back. The first week I spent at my parents' house and the next at my in-laws' house. They pampered me as if I was a small baby. But I felt guilty for being treated that way. Their sympathy was genuine but I didn't need it. I just needed their support and thus, I announced that I was moving to my own place, a rented apartment in Saket. I had asked my manager in Economic Times to see if he could arrange for an official transfer and he tried to do his best. I got a job in the same firm but in a different branch in Saket.

'Would you like some tea?' I asked.

'Yes, I would love that. Sunita and my daughter will be joining us soon.'

Dikshit, Darsh's brother, had helped me set up my new house. I was glad that he had been so nice to me. When I first told my mother-in-law about my decision to stay alone, she was a little apprehensive, not because she hoped that I would stay with her but because she was worried about my survival alone. But when I convinced her that I needed that space, she understood. Honestly, after Darsh, I didn't have much to talk about with his family. I wasn't intending on distancing myself but as my mother always said- I wasn't good at anything, even keeping up with relationships, I guess!

'So, Adah, all set for a new journey?' asked Sunita, my sister-in-law.

'I think so. I just have to work on my bedroom a little,' I answered.

'Should I give you a hand in unpacking those boxes? We can split the work and your room will be ready soon,' she offered.

'That's very kind of you. I am sorry but my life now depends on those boxes. Those are the only memories of Darsh I am left with! I want to take my own time to absorb the sorrow and find happiness in this new place. Please don't mind.'

'I can understand how difficult it must be for you. Don't worry. I will leave you to it. But promise me that you will let me know if you need anything. I am just a call away.'

'Of course. Thank you for all the help and support,' I smiled.

'Come on, don't be so formal. We are a family.'

That night, I plugged in my earphones and played sad mashups on repeat. I wanted to let it all out. Just like how a dam prevents the water from overflowing, I think the old place acted as a barrier for me. It prevented me from letting it all out. I was angry at Darsh. I was sad. I was broken. And all that needed a good repair. Opening of those boxes allowed my eyes to begin leaking and the whole night was spent in the company of pictures, memories, songs and alcohol. My insomnia found the moonlight as its sole companion and with that, my soul also found new buddies to hang out with. All by myself, I would return home from work and watch a movie, cook dinner and then head straight to bed. Weekends were no different. I just had more time for myself during the day.

It was after a month of solitude which I had started liking that my mother and my father visited my place. Looking at the clean, dust-free shelves and immaculate rooms, my mother praised me. That was something unusual because she normally refrained from showering words of appreciation.

'Your house looks so good. You are holding up quite fine, aren't you?'

'Oh, yes, I am. Thank you. Work has been really promising. I might even get a promotion soon.'

'So what plans do you have for your birthday?'

'Nothing special, Ma. I might take the day off, chill at home. Maybe bake a cake and watch a movie.'

'What? That's not right. You will have to come to our place and we will have a small celebration. That's final.'

'No, Ma. I don't want to have a party. Please don't insist on socializing. I am happy like this.'

'I am not here to listen to your ifs and buts. Your father and I will plan everything. We will ask Darsh's family to come and stay for some time.'

'Darsh's father wouldn't be able to. He prefers being in his own house because of his mobility issue and I think mummy will also prefer staying at home,' I interrupted.

'Which means that you are fine with the idea of the party?'

'I didn't say that. Come on, Ma. I am not a child any more that you are now forcing me to host a party,' I tried to present a reasonable argument.

'Keep quiet. The party idea is on. We will make all the arrangements. You just come home on time.'

I couldn't argue with my mother. She was so adamant. My birthday was a week away and the thought of meeting people who would try to share my sorrow by their ambiguous questions scared me. I didn't want to be a part of any discussion that aroused pity for me. But who would dare explain my dilemma to my mother!

I had to buy a dress for the party and thus, I decided to leave the office early on a Tuesday and head to Sarojini market. I didn't want any company because the company meant more time to be wasted in the market bargaining about trivial items that were not the priority. I hated shopping. Walking alone, looking at the shops in the narrow lanes of the market, I came across a big shop that had all women's things. I thought of checking it out. When I asked the person behind the counter to show me an evening dress, he went to another small storeroom and came back with plenty of options.

What caught my eyes was a greenish-blue dress that was made from a satiny material. As I tried it on, the creamy sheets of the dress slipped through my shoulders, peppering my body with soft and tender kisses. Darsh would have liked it, I thought to myself. His favourite colour was green and this was the exact kind of dress that he had bought for me the previous year on Valentine's Day. The cute thin black border on the mini sleeves made the dress even prettier. I didn't have to think again before selecting it. I bought it for my birthday.

'Happy Birthday,' everyone shouted unanimously. I took a good five minutes to look at every face in the room. Other than my loved ones, there were several other people in the room.

'Hi, Adah. Happy Birthday,' said Pranit lowering a glass of champagne towards me.

'Thanks. I am sorry but I don't want to get drunk today.'

'Come on, it's your birthday. It's time to celebrate.' He persisted.

'Please, Pranit.' He got the hint and moved away to talk to Aadrika.

I paced through the room and caught hold of my father by his arm.

'Pa, can I talk to you for a second?' I excused him.

'Yes, dear. What happened? Are you enjoying yourself?'

'What is Pranit doing here? Why would you invite Mrs Gupta and her son? I don't even know them properly.' I sounded frustrated.

'She is a good friend of your mother that's why your mother might have invited her. Why are you worried?'

'Because I don't want to indulge in any conversation with Pranit but he is trying to talk to me. It's awkward.'

'That's good, you know. He broke up with his girlfriend. So, he is single at the moment.'

I didn't understand what my father said. When I did, I threw the glass of juice that was in my hand. It crashed on the wall, spilling juice all over the furry rug that guarded the dining area. There was pin-drop silence in the room. No one spoke. No one moved. With tears in my eyes, I stormed out of the door, waited outside for the cab to come and went straight home. Not even bothering to check how my parents would have handled the situation, I kept to myself for a week. I didn't attend their calls nor did I answer their messages. I was hurt. I couldn't believe that they were hoping to set me up with Pranit, that spineless man who couldn't even take a stand for his love.

'Why are you here?' I asked my mother when she visited me after a few days.

'You need to think rationally. Can I at least come in?' she asked.

I couldn't say no, could I? After comfortably seating herself on the sofa, my mother spoke words that twisted my internals to such an extent that my soul was ready to leave my body for good.

'You have to think about what you did that day. It was completely irrational of you to leave the party like that. We are thinking of your good. You are just 30 and this is a ripe age. You need to start your life again. It is too early for you to give up on love. Pranit is a nice boy and he belongs to the same community as ours. His family is quite well-to-do and he plans to settle here in Delhi. See, everything in our favour. Then what problem do you have?'

'I cannot believe you. You don't understand, do you? The problem is that my love for Darsh cannot just vanish into thin air just because he is not there with me. His memories are enough for me and I don't need another man in my life to continue living my life. I am happy the way my life is turning out to be. Can we please just drop the topic?'

'No, this not something that can be dropped just like that. Your decisions have been impacting our lives in the worst possible way. Do you think anyone would marry your sister when they will come to know that her elder sister is a young widow and lives alone? Do you seriously think that they are not going to wonder that something is seriously wrong with you or that you are a...'

'Cut me some slack, Ma. Do you realize that you are talking to your daughter? Why do you always question my choice? Right from my childhood, I have always been a victim of your sardonic comments because you think that I cannot do anything on my own. If you try to see it clearly, I have been quite happy with my choices.'

'Yes? Happy with your choices? You opted for a wrong course, wasted our money because you wanted to become a writer. Have you become one yet because it has been 9 years since you left college? You married Darsh going against our wish of marrying Pranit and see now, Darsh is no longer with you. You went to New York to do that training. What help has that given you so far?'

'You don't understand at all and I am tired of arguing with you. I am a writer in a Newspaper company. I edit and I proofread the writeups before they are printed in the paper. It is a dignified job. If you are waiting for my name to be printed in the paper, it would take a lot of time because becoming a writer is not easy. And stop blaming my choice of marrying Darsh. It was the best decision I ever made.'

'You are acting like a fool. How do you plan on spending time alone for another 40-50 years? Isn't that a long time?'

'I want to ask you just one question and I want you to be honest with your answer. Why do you want me to settle down again? Have I ever complained that I am lonely or sad?'

'I am your mother. I understand the pain that you are going through. I also understand that it is not easy to be alone and spend time with memories. It will impact your overall being and the result will not be good.'

I felt a tinge of happiness because my mother's words proved that she cared for me enough and that she thought about me when I was not with her. However, upon further discussion, she proved my notions about her wrong.

'There is another reason as well,' she blurted.

'And what might that be?'

'Since the party, everyone who meets me or your father has been asking us to think about your future and not do something that will not let us die in peace. A young widow cannot survive alone for long and thus, it is imperative to remove this label from your name. If you marry Pranit, it will be a win-win for all of us. You get a husband and, in some time, you can bear children. We will also be happy because we will have an answer for all those embarrassing questions.'

'Oh, now I understand. It is not about me. It has never been about me. You have always tried to undermine my choices because you are so worried about what others would say.

Well, good news- I am not going to listen to whatever you are saying.'

'How is that good news?'

'It is because I am not going to live here with you all anymore. I will shift to someplace that will be too far that you will think twice before visiting me. I didn't know that my sorrow was such a problem for you. You and Pa are not even allowing me to grieve the death of my husband. It has only been one and a half years and you want me to forget everything and remarry. What do you think I am? Don't I have emotions?'

The verbal battle went on for another hour. I had never felt so left out in my entire life. I wanted to just move away from all the chaos. My mother left my house by evening and she warned me before stepping outside.

'Think about it. We are not wrong but you are. You better do as we say or we will break all ties with you. Enough of your 'my choice, my decisions' drama.'

It had come to that- breaking off the ties because I didn't want to remarry. I spent the restless night thinking about what I could do and there lay only one door open for me- New York. I could get a job at NYT and permanently shift there. Yes, permanently moving away from the only people whom I could call close was a big decision and if things didn't work out, I would be doomed. Yet I was willing to take the risk. Maybe because I had realized with time that the journey wasn't so much about becoming anything but about unbecoming everything that I was not.

I called up Lina the next day and explained everything to her. She tried to convince me to think about the decision again because it was a big one but I knew my mind too well. All I had to do after that was to wait for my fate to decide.

In another month, I got a call from Lina confirming my job in NYT. I was expected to join in two weeks. The only change was that my family wasn't supportive of my decision, yet again and that I couldn't live with Lina anymore. I had to find a permanent settlement. My flight was supposed to take off three days later. Even such less time seemed quite enough for me to pack the essentials and be ready.

Finally, the D day came. I went to Darsh's parents' house first. They weren't supportive of my decision either. But at least they kept all those long speeches at bay. My father-in-law and my mother-in-law gave me blessings and promised to be there whenever I needed them. Sunita was all teary-eyed. She had prepared pickle for me. Her daughter was at her grandmother's and so I couldn't meet her. I then went to my parents' house and the unwelcoming vibe just put me in the black mood. No one spoke to me except Aadrika, who spoke words of discouragement. Within 15 minutes, I left for the airport, anxious and nervous at the same time.

I began work in October 2015 and since then New York has become my life. I have a few friends in the office but I don't like to meet them post office hours. Call it my eccentric nature or the fact that I am selectively social, mingling for no good reason is still not my cup of tea. I worked quite hard the previous year so that I could be promoted to the post of Senior Editor. Things did seem to work in my favour. My family didn't call for a year. Aadrika called some time back to inform me that she was moving to New York for her college. We didn't meet nor did we speak about anything else. It has been the same since then. Once in a while,

Darsh's mother calls me but we hardly talk for more than 15 minutes. I was quite happy at that moment with how my life was progressing. Love seemed like a distant dream. Work, however, was a pleasure- something that kept me going. It was going well till a new employee in NYT began irking me by trying to initiate conversation. I tried to give a clear sign that I wasn't interested and that helped him realize that I was the wrong bait.

III
AVYAN

21

Scratching the Surface

I felt the floor slipping away from beneath my feet. Bobby was left rooted to the spot. It wasn't rocket science for Cole to figure out what I had in my mind or rather in my heart. She was quick to offer me a glass of water before my emotions could drown the pain that I felt. Choking over water, I managed to ask just one question- 'Is she married?'

'Of course, she is married. How could you not see this?'

'How am I supposed to see it? She doesn't roam around wearing a label saying so,' I knew I sounded foolish.

'Yes, but didn't you ever think that how could a girl like her not be with anyone?'

Cole's point did make sense but my mind refused to believe that. In another moment, Cole's phone rang.

'Yes, hi. How is it going? Where are you?' she asked the person on the other side of the phone and then continued, 'Yes, I will be there. Just give me ten minutes.' She cut the call to face me. Putting her hand on my shoulder, she gave me a sympathizing look.

'Look, Avyan, if you are thinking that she would be interested in having a relationship, then you are wrong. I can tell you one thing for sure that she is quite happy with her life. If you try to express your feelings for her, you might repel her further. She looks at you as a good friend and nothing more than that.'

Tanny was sensible and intelligent. She had told me to do the right thing. But she didn't know that my heart was a victim of the Cupid. It did exactly the opposite, for it couldn't bear the thought of staying away from Adah. Talking to Adah that day would have been like digging my own grave; hence, I decided to wait for a while before confronting her. Adah had not given any hint that could convince me that she was drawn towards me. I still knew half of the story. I had to find out more about her, about her family and her marriage. Tanny had just told me that her husband was not with her. Were they divorced? If yes, then why would Adah dress to the nines and celebrate that day? If no, where was her husband? More importantly, who was her husband?

'Bobby, I need your help. I need you to throw a party at your place and invite everyone, including Adah,' I declared.

'Why would I do that? Has Peter decided to promote me or what?'

'You will do that because you are happy and you want to be grateful to all your friends,' I explained.

'The fact that no one understands you doesn't imply that you are an artist!' He jibed.

'What's wrong with you? I want to meet Adah and I cannot simply ask her to go out with me.'

'And that's why you want me to spend more than 500 bucks and organize a party! How clever you are!'

'Listen, I cannot come up with any other excuse. I need to get her talking so that I know what's wrong and where my love stands!'

'Let me think of a better excuse then because your mind is like the school in the summertime- no class, no kids, nothing!'

'What are you trying to say- that I am stupid?' I chastised.

'No, no. I am not saying that. I am just saying that you just have bad luck when thinking,' he laughed.

Looking at me with those squinted eyes, Bobby didn't take long to gather that I was pissed off. He told me to head back to my desk and meet him again during the lunchtime. By then he was sure that he would be able to come up with something.

We met at the cafeteria during lunchtime and Bobby seemed quite excited.

'Rather than throwing a party for those whom I don't know, I would rather advise you to ask her to lunch. You can begin the conversation there,' he suggested.

'Not a good idea. The moment she gets to know that I am trying to get her to like me or the sorts, she is going to flip out. Not only will this end my prospect of asking her out but will also ruin the friendship that I have with her.'

'That makes sense. Should I come with you? Will that help? Maybe she will think it is a friendly lunch and I can save you when your mouth will go out of control,' he asked.

'That sounds like a plan. Should I call her now then?'

'Yes, but wait. Let me call her.'

I knew Bobby was right. Asking Adah to come over for lunch would be successful only when she came and that would happen if Bobby initiated the plan. Fortunately, Adah agreed and within 15 minutes, the three of us were binging on the Pizza that we had ordered. Though it could not match up the one that Capizzi offered yet it was better than the minced chicken.

'Hi. Where were you yesterday?' I asked Adah.

'Nothing. I just had some work at home. What's up with you both? How come you invited me for lunch today?' she queried.

'If we could, we would invite you every day,' I paused saying that because I realized what had just escaped my mouth. Nervous and sweaty, I turned towards Bobby who was grinning from ear to ear.

'He means to say that it is mostly the two of us who eat together. So, we thought why not ask you to join us. You know, for a change!' Bobby's proud save was evident in his speech. He didn't even flounder once. It was like he had come prepared for that.

'Well, thanks for inviting me. Anyway, I wasn't doing much and I desperately needed some company to distract my mind from the continuous squabbling of Brenda.'

'Brenda? Brenda of the 13th floor?' I stammered.

'Yes, Brenda of the 13th floor. Why do you ask?'

'Well, Brenda and I didn't quite start on a good note,' I admitted.

'Oh, yes, she couldn't change your mood, could she?' Adah broke into a hysterical laugh.

My cheeks were tomato red with embarrassment. Brenda was a loudmouth! She had made me look like a fool before Adah.

'That's alright. I cannot deny but I admire your honesty with which you didn't reciprocate her move!'

For a moment I thought she was serious. But then she laughed again and I realized my foolery!

'Listen, you two, my sister is coming to New York for a week to visit me. Adah, will you help her out with shopping as I am not very good at that?' Bobby asked.

'Of course! I would love that. I don't have many friends here so I am always on the lookout for a company for shopping.'

'Why no friends? Your parents? Siblings?'

Adah was awkward for a moment but Bobby's presence did the magic. She couldn't leave the conversation just like that and thus, she spoke.

'They are all back in India.'

'Do you have a sibling too?'

'Yes, I have a younger sister, Aadrika.'

'Wow! Is she married?' Bobby joked. Frightened what his question would lead to, I gulped fear. But to my surprise, Adah took it lightly. I wondered why she was always uncomfortable talking to me about all that. Had she figured out that I was in love with her? Or was it too much that I was thinking?

'No, she isn't married. But sadly for you, she is in a relationship.' Bobby pretended to be sad and devastated by the news! I couldn't help but look at Adah and her charm.

'What about you, Avyan? Do you have any siblings?' Adah inquired.

'Oh, yes. I have a younger sister, Nandita. Bobby has met her already. She came to New York some time back for her internship.'

'Oh really? Did she train under Susan?' she was quick to ask.

'Yes, Susan. How do you know her?'

'Susan was my trainer too. I had done an internship here a long time back before getting a job here. She had assigned me a project under Judith.'

'Oh, wow! So how long have you been working here?' I asked.

'Three years in a row. Before that, I worked here for a year.'

'Why did you take a break then? Did you switch the job?' Bobby intervened sensing trouble.

'Oh, yes. I had to return to India. I had to get married.' Saying that Adah's forehead developed lines that seemed deeper than the natural gorges.

'What? You are married? And I was thinking of wooing you soon,' Bobby cajoled to release the tension in the atmosphere.

'Why? What happened to your Sam?' Adah asked.

'How do you know about Sam?'

Adah gestured towards me and Bobby hit me on my arm in an attempt to take revenge. I wanted to ask her what happened to her husband but Bobby's wink was a clear warning. It was like we were playing 'House of Cards'. One wrong move would have resulted in tumbling down of the entire structure.

'Aah! Sam and I broke up long back. She was a gold digger. I wonder how I could be so lousy in identifying a person,' said Bobby.

'Don't worry. You will get your soulmate soon,' consoled Adah.

'What about you? Are you planning to explore love outside the boundaries of marriage?'

There it was- the bombshell! Bobby had asked the most dreaded question. I was sure that she wouldn't answer that and I waited for her to get up and storm off like they show in the movies.

'No, not really. I am quite happy you know!' Her smile convinced Bobby that he could go on with that game.

'That's not fair. How can you be happy? Marriages are meant to make people suffer, especially men. Don't you agree with me, Avy?'

'Yes, absolutely.' I expressed my agreement.

'That's not true. My husband is happy. I mean 'was' happy,' she spoke grimly.

'Why? What happened? Why did you just change the tense?' I asked, finally mustering some courage.

'He passed away in an accident four and a half years ago.'

What followed next was Bobby's creepy talk about how his sister only likes those men who wear polished shoes. I knew very well what he was trying to do. The lunchtime got extended by half an hour but that was fine as I had just discovered the secret that prevented Adah from being in a relationship.

22

The Face-off

While Bobby urged me to ask Adah for a movie, I knew he was asking me to bite more than I could chew. After the first lunch that the three of us had together, Adah started hanging out with us more often than before. She laughed with her heart when she heard Bobby chatter. With me, it was more of a formal conversation. It wasn't so because she was awkward. It was so because I felt awkward. Bobby tried to make me a part of hilarious conversation time and again, but I knew my sense of humour went out for a walk every time Adah sat before me.

'Bobby, what should I do? I try to think of funny conversations yet I am not able to talk to Adah. She must be thinking that I am a fool!' I coaxed Bobby to help me.

'Don't let your mind wander- it is far too small to be let out on its own.'

'Can you, for once, be serious?' I fretted.

'What? I am telling the truth! You are awful when you have to talk to women. Accept that, will you?'

I knew he wasn't lying. But I needed things to pace up between Adah and me. I couldn't even say if she liked me.

'I have another ace up my sleeve. Do you care to listen?'

'Yes, of course. What is it?' I jumped with joy.

'I invited Adah for dinner tomorrow with the three of us.' He beamed.

'Three? Has your brain gone on a vacation?' I basked in the glory of my first ever sarcastic comment!

'You do realize that a touch-up of foundation won't conceal your stupidity, don't you?' He won again. Easily! 'Jade is the one joining us!'

Jade was Bobby's sister. He was clever enough to invite his sister so that Adah did not feel awkward. There was no doubt that the drinks would be served. Hence, the plan was to indulge in a serious conversation with Adah and get to know her opinion about re-marriage.

The next day, my mind was not in the right place. Peter screamed at me twice for bringing in the wrong file into his cabin. Fortunately, his wife was held up at the airport and hence, her calls kept saving me from his wrath.

'Hey, Avy, now that you are in no mood to work, I want you to do something for me,' insisted Peter.

The sudden demand brought out a deep frown on my forehead. I knew it was not going to be good. Time was moving at snail's pace before Peter opened his Pandora box!

'My wife has been held up at the airport. She needs her driving license and her birth certificate. Since your brain needs some time off, why don't you give your legs a nice exercise, eh?'

'You want me to go to the airport now?' I asked, perplexed.

'Yes, why? Is there a problem?'

'It is 6 in the evening. I have plans for dinner, Peter,' I tried to explain.

'Well, it's not like you cannot have dinner if you are a little late, is it? Now, come on, hurry up.'

I had no choice than to run errands for my boss. Otherwise, he would have found a reason not to promote me. Not that I was hoping for a promotion but still, I didn't want to provoke the odds to begin blocking my path.

Bobby's call alerted me of the time. It was 8:30 pm and the three guests for the night were waiting for me in Mercato, the Italian restaurant.

'Where are you?' asked Bobby.

'On the way. There is so much traffic. I will be there in another 15 minutes. Okay?'

'Yes, come soon.'

When I reached the venue, the girls were binging on celery Bloody Mary. Jade looked pale as if she was about to puke but Adah looked sober still.

'Hey, how are you? I am so sorry for keeping you waiting,' I spoke to Adah in whispers.

'Hey, come on. I am not the only one waiting here!'

Red with embarrassment, I moved opposite to Adah and sat down. It took half an hour to get into the mood of a serious conversation. Bobby, as usual, began.

'I feel so lonely at times. Even though Sam loved my money more than me, I still had someone who loved me. I miss her. Oh God, help me find love!'

'That's not true, Bob. We all love you though in a different way,' Adah was careful with her words.

'Tell me, doesn't it get lonely at times, especially when you are away from the chaos of life, alone and in solitude? Don't you miss that special someone who would listen to all that you have to say without judging you or making you feel small? Don't you miss the warmth of the arms that hold you when the world seems scary?'

There was absolute silence at the table. I could see a tiny drop of tear escaping the corner of Adah's right eye. She kept staring at her glass as if it were about to say something. Her index finger traced the boundary of the glass. The reddish cocktail swaying with the movement of the glass didn't perturb her thoughts. Just then, a subtle smile escaped her lips and for some odd reason, I did not have a very good feeling about it.

'What happened? What made you smile?' I asked.

'It's nothing.' She paused for a brief moment.

'Oh, come on, Adah. We all are friends here. You can tell us,' persuaded Jade.

'I just remembered Darsh. I miss him so much. Yes, Bobby, it is difficult to live with only the memories but I wouldn't say it is impossible. At times like these, when I get a chance to remember my sweet moments with my husband, I get to cherish those lost moments! That's what keeps you going, you know!'

'That's true. But have you ever thought of what you would do if you find love again? Unlike me, who is desperately waiting for someone special to replace Sam, I am sure you would have thought about it more seriously!'

'Of course, I have. But my heart just refuses to accept that thought. I have come to realize that I don't wish to fall in love again. I am happy the way things are at the moment. Just because someone is no longer with you, it doesn't mean that you replace their place with someone who can be with you.'

'Don't you think this is a one-dimensional perspective?' I asked.

'If you don't agree with me, think about those children who lose one of their parents at a very young age. It is very rare when the other parent decides to remarry. And how do they survive without having someone around? With the pleasant memories that they hold in their heart forever.'

'I am sorry but do not agree with you. Everyone deserves a second chance. And life without love is like sending back the opportunity without even inviting it in!'

'Avyan, different strokes for different folks! I do not deny what you are saying. It is just that I will never be ready to replace Darsh's love with someone else's.'

'You are being unfair to your heart then,' I maintained.

'I am not. And why are you taking this so personally?'

'I don't know. Maybe because I know someone who adores you but you are so unapproachable that he isn't able to find the right time to talk to you about his feelings,' I admitted.

'Is that someone you?'

I was taken by surprise. Her expressions gave the hint that it was a statement and not a question. She knew that I was drawn towards her yet she didn't say anything for so long.

Thanks to the alcohol that she was approachable that day. Bobby and Jade had taken a back seat after their mission had initiated successfully. I didn't need Bobby's help at that juncture. It would either be a miss or a hit. It looked like a miss though!

'Yes, that someone is me,' I said in one breath and waited for her to respond.

'I could figure out. I am surprised you waited so long to tell me.'

'How do you know about this?' I asked.

'It was quite evident, Avyan. The way you initiated the conversation during the ball and then you tried your best to reach out to me. I am sorry that I was always unapproachable. Maybe it was because I was looking for friendship and I realized pretty soon that we both expected different things.'

'Adah, I just want you to think about it. I will not argue the toss with you. I just want you to think about it once. Is that too much to ask?'

'Come on, you both. Don't spoil the evening with your emotional melodrama! Avy, you are not good when it comes to women. If you still don't believe me, you should get your brain checked,' Bobby stammered, the alcohol clearly taking over his conscience.

'I think we need to take these two home,' suggested Adah.

'Yes, you are right. You take a cab and I shall drop these two on my way back home. Will it be fine?'

'Are you sure you don't want me to accompany you?'

'I would love that but then it would get late and nearly unsafe for you to go back to your place alone,' I added.

'Thank you for being so thoughtful. Avyan, I don't want to hurt you. It is just that…'

My dejected expression might have cut her short, for she changed the course of her dialogue at that very instant.

'…okay, I will think about it. Shall we leave?'

'Yes, we should. Can you hail a cab for us too?' I asked.

That night, even though the discussion didn't come to fruition, it was special. I could talk my heart out and express what I felt before Adah. Bobby, however, had another opinion. According to him, Adah was the hero as she already knew about her secret lover. He was right but I couldn't admit that before him, could I? That would have given him another reason to mock me.

Breaking my reverie, Scarlet jumped onto me and started licking my face. She never missed that. And I loved how she always showed me that she adored me. It struck my brilliant mind just then that I hadn't expressed my feelings to Adah. Yes, she already knew that I 'adored' her but it wouldn't matter unless she heard it from the horse's mouth! I decided to confront her again the next day during lunch. I messaged Bobby to call me once his senses are back and just when I pressed the button, my phone rang.

'Are you sure that you are in your senses?' I asked.

'Of course! It has been three hours since I came back home. I am fine now. Tell me what happened,' he articulated.

'Adah is a little apprehensive of giving herself a second chance,' I said.

'That's not true. If you ask your heart, you will get the answer. She is not looking for a second chance and she knows this too well. However much you try to convince her, it is very less likely that she will budge.'

'I think you are right. What should I do then? I cannot give up on her this easily. At least, let me make an effort,' I reasoned.

'You are right. We need to find out a little more about her first. Let me fix a meeting with Tanny. Maybe she will be able to help us here.'

Though the idea didn't guarantee success, it was still something to look forward to. Tanny had known Adah for quite many years. She would know about her family and her notions.

I couldn't sleep that night. It seemed like my insomnia and the moonlight were in a long-distance relationship. They wanted to spend the time together and thus, my baggy eyes bore the brunt of their decision.

23

An Unexpected Epiphany

"Our notions about happiness entrap us. We forget that they are just ideas. Our idea of happiness can prevent us from actually being happy. We fail to see the opportunity for joy that is right in front of us when we are caught in a belief that happiness should take a particular form."

— *Thich Nhat Hanh*

Life changes. You lose love. You lose family. You lose friends. You lose trust as well. You lose pieces of yourself that you never imagined would be gone. And then, without you even realizing it, these pieces come back. Like how you get the answer after leaving the examination hall! New love enters. New bonds are formed. New friends come along. And a stronger, wiser you is staring back in the mirror. No matter how bad it gets, better days are always waiting, hoping you will make it there to accept the gift of smiles and joy that life has to offer. But that doesn't mean that you will not have any more woes and weal. Those are the part and parcel of nature and thus, they remain with you forever.

What Adah felt couldn't be understood by me because I wasn't sailing in the same boat. I had had my share of troubles when I was young. Not a bright student at all, I always flunked in more than three subjects and my father had to use the rod because he didn't believe in sparing the child. However much I tried to study Chemistry and Physics, the concepts never found a firm base in my head. I struggled with the equations and the memorization part. Yet when it came to opting for subjects in the 11th grade, I opted for Science along with Mathematics. My father was unhappy with my performance in the board exams in which I scored 60% yet my mother's belief in me encouraged me to pursue a Master's degree in Journalism.

My sister, Nandita, was always a bright student. She scored the highest marks in all the subjects and was also good in literary activities. She was eloquent and poised. I was shabby when I had to go up on stage. Public Speaking was a distant dream for me. However, the numbers and statistics always fascinated me. My mother and my sister always supported every endeavour of mine. But my father didn't quite see eye to eye with me. Nevertheless, I was driven and motivated enough to carve a niche for myself. My life wasn't as interesting as Adah's but it did have a few roadblocks like my breakup with my classmate in college whom I dearly loved, the death of my close friend and the lack of affection that I could see in Adah's eyes. Though I moved on pretty quickly because of devoting all my attention to my work, I still had a vacant spot in my heart that couldn't be replaced by anyone. At times, when I am alone, the pangs of guilt and loneliness hurt my soul like a thousand spears piercing through the mere fabric of my existence. Yet somehow, I manage to cope with the situation. It was only here in New York that the pain had reduced considerably owing to two different reasons- one, I had my dream job and two, I thought Adah was the missing piece of my heart's jigsaw. How was I to know that we both were star-crossed lovers, each battling with a different storm differently! While I was lovelorn when it came to Adah, she, too, was ill-fated because she lost her true love too soon.

Revealing the turbulence in my love-life was the biggest mistake I had done so far because my mother couldn't fathom the fact that I was going bananas over a widow (that's the language she often used) and my father had found another reason to call me a disgrace to the family. My sister, on the contrary, took my side and tried convincing my mother. Even though she hadn't had any conversation with Adah, she had seen her with Susan and Adah's personality had impressed her. But nothing can convince a mother's heart. While my mother was worried about me marrying a foreigner, here I was telling her how much I loved Adah. At that juncture, I felt my mother would have agreed easily had I told her that a foreigner would become her daughter-in-law.

Things were not well at that moment. Adah didn't seem comfortable in my presence anymore and before taking a step forward and trying to convince her, I had to gather all the prior knowledge about her. The next day in office was slow even though the workload was immense. Bobby and I decided to meet Tanny Cole at the restaurant right opposite to our office building. Judging by the way Cole initiated the conversation, I knew for sure that she was well aware of the agenda.

'Thanks a lot, Tanny. It means a lot to us that you agreed to meet us.' Bobby, as always, hosted the show.

'That's alright. I think I know why you wanted to meet me. Is this about Adah?' she asked.

'Yes! This idiot here has fallen in love with her and when he expressed his feelings towards her, Adah right away refused. No amount of convincing would melt her heart. And that's why we wanted you to tell us a little more about her so that Avy can try his luck again.'

'Well, I feel sad for you, Avyan. You are a nice man. But you fell in love with the wrong person indeed!' Tanny confessed, a serious expression evident on her white face.

'The damage has already been done. I ask you to help me. Please tell me about her family. Didn't they ever think about her remarriage?' I enquired.

'Of course, they did. See, the flaw lies in her family dynamics. Her family doesn't really see eye to eye with her. Her sister, too, doesn't take her side even when Adah is right. She is just so much into herself. They are not bad people. It is just that Adah always felt the hollow in her heart- the hollow of not being understood. While all her friends were being supported in their respective homes, she felt dejected because her parents didn't understand her desire to become a writer nor did they understand why she wanted to marry Darsh, her husband.'

'Even my father has a problem with everything that I do but that doesn't mean that I shut myself from all the pleasures of life. Don't you think she is being unfair to herself?'

'No, no, it's not that. She is not being unfair at all. When she was in college, she met Darsh during the first year of her college. He was her senior and they both didn't waste time to realize that what they had was not friendship alone. Very often when I spoke to her about him, I saw an uncanny brightness in her eyes. She believed in him because he was the only person who never undermined her dreams and desires. You know, she was very happy with him. And whenever she remembers that fateful day, the day he met with an accident, her eyes well up and she cries inconsolably.'

'But there will come a time when she will have to move on, isn't it?' asked Bobby.

'Yes, it is imperative for her to let go of the past and make some new memories. But I also feel that if the past is not holding her back, then why should she be forced to make new memories?'

'Why doesn't she talk to her parents?' I asked.

'I have tried asking her many times. Her sister is in the same city, yet whenever I bring up the topic of meeting her sister, she politely digresses from it and excuses herself. I am sure it must be something related to Darsh. She wouldn't share with anyone!'

Sighing in hopelessness, I gazed at the sky. It was clear. Symbolically that would indicate positivity yet I doubted the relevance of symbolism! Tanny told us about how Adah had decided against her parents' wish to come and settle in New York and how since then she had never spoken to them. But something was amiss. Why would she decide to settle here? There was a link missing and that made it difficult for me to connect the dots. I spent the night caressing Scarlet and thinking about a way to come clear before Adah. Before the clock struck 5 in the morning, I decided that that was something I had to do on my own. I had to stop taking Bobby's help and had to face Adah on my own. Resolute yet hesitant, I messaged Adah at 6 in the morning asking her to meet me at Cappizi, for I had to discuss something important. Just when I pressed the 'send' button, I heard a loud cry. Rushing towards the kitchen, I feared the unanticipated. Scarlet had dropped the bowl of cucumber on herself and a piece of glass had pierced into her paw. Tiny drops of blood started oozing out from the little paw and it scared the daylights out of me. I rang the nearest veterinary hospital only to find that there was no doctor available. Panicking at the situation at hand, I dialled Bobby's number and asked him to help. He connected me with his sister who had a dog. She guided me and helped me remove the piece of glass and bandage Scarlet's paw. The first thing I had to do the next morning was to take Scarlet to the vet lest there was any pus formation.

That night, I had several things running in my mind- Scarlet was in pain and I couldn't bear her occasional moaning, I had to prepare myself to talk to Adah and I kept on thinking about how my life was progressing. It felt as if I was standing at a juncture from where each road seemed to lead into a labyrinth. No one could hold my hand and walk with me. Whatever decisions I had to take would determine the course of my life and I would solely be responsible for what I choose. It sounded dangerous! It was risky for sure. Adah hadn't confirmed about our meeting yet and that thought kept me awake. I wondered if she would even see my face again. But somewhere deep inside I knew I hadn't done anything wrong- nothing to hurt her. I was just trying to get to know her reasons and beliefs. That's all or was it?

24

If Truth Be Told

Scarlet's paw was fine. It was a minor injury but she still seemed to be in a lot of pain. Hence, I had to make sure that I crushed her tablets (a painkiller majorly and an antibiotic), mixed them homogeneously with the milk and then gave them to her. However smart she thought she was, my trick did fool her and she was comforted by the aftereffect of the medicine. Seeing her pain vanish, I was ready to leave for office. Peter had given me another document to proofread and change according to the need. It was another proposal and I hadn't worked on it owing to my dilemma. I had to speak clearly with Adah or else my house of cards would not remain in place; it would soon shatter if I kept ignoring my work requirements.

Dusting my bicycle, I pedalled as fast as possible to reach the office a little early and finish the pending assignment. When I entered my cubicle, I found Adah sitting on my chair with her back facing me. I could see a magazine in her hand. Gulping down the sudden awkwardness, I greeted her and asked her the reason why she had come up to my office.

'I wanted to talk to you. Last night did not go well. I tried to make you understand my point of view but I knew I had failed. I do not want to lose a friend because of the misunderstanding. Can we talk?'

I hesitated not because I didn't want to talk but because Peter eyed me from the corner of his room.

'Can you pretend to be talking to me regarding a marketing proposal? Peter is watching us and he seems to be more interested in having a conversation with you.' I maintained my calm and hoped that she followed my cue.

Adah, no doubt, created such a realistic facade that even Peter was forced to ask me if she had come to meet me to discuss something really important.

'You tell me if you need anything, okay?' He said patting my back.

'I surely will. Let's see how this goes.'

'Why don't you take her out for lunch. The two of you can talk about it over lunch. By the way, what is the entire discussion about?' He finally threw the bombshell.

I took a good one minute to rehearse the made-up situation in my mind and then blurted out, 'She wanted my help in landing Frisco Furnishings. She is already writing about them in the upcoming print edition and thus, wanted to know if the marketing team can help her land them in NYT. They are a blue-chip company, you know!'

'Of course, I know. Huh, she thought of this only now. I have been thinking about Frisco for a long time. These young minds are not so bright now, are they?' Peter couldn't help but boast about an idea or belief that was non-existent.

I avoided nodding in affirmation as then the joke would be on me. Since Peter had bought what I had offered him, it took me hardly any more time to leave the office and meet Adah in the park nearby.

'What you said the other day was right. You were never disrespectful nor were you clingy. You just tried to reach out to me. It was my fault that I did not come clear before you right in the beginning. But I wasn't sure if I was right in my judgement!'

'Forget all that. I understand that you had to do what you had to do. Still, I would like to know more about why you settled here. Didn't your parents ask you to stay back in India after Darsh passed away?' I feared the outcome. It was like removing the bandage from a fresh wound. You wouldn't know if it would start bleeding. Her wound was not old either.

She waited. For a long time. We chewed on our lunch in the meantime and then she finally spoke.

'When Darsh passed away, we were living in Mumbai. Alone. After all the funeral formalities were done, I asked my parents and my in-laws to go back, for I wanted to be alone. They didn't agree but eventually had to give in. I wasn't depressed. I was sad and to accept that Darsh was no longer with me in flesh and blood, I needed the time alone. It was after some months when I shifted back to Delhi. First, I stayed with my in-laws and then with my parents. It didn't work because they tried to convince me to remarry. That was out of the question. After much thinking, I knew one thing for sure that love was not on the cards for me. I did not need that. I needed something else. I wanted to pursue my passion and live with the love I once possessed. It might sound weird, I know. My parents thought the same.'

'It does sound weird. You could have given yourself some time before shunning yourself out from the world.'

'It is not that, Avyan. The reason why I came here and left my parents behind is that they were not able to understand me. It is not always important to follow the usual or expected course of action. That is so stereotypical.'

'You haven't talked to them ever since, have you?' I asked.

'I do, once in two months maybe. I speak to my father because he is good at avoiding discussions. My mother never leaves a chance to give me a lecture on how to live a happy and fulfilling life.'

'What about your sister? Where does she live?'

'She lives in the same city. We hardly meet. Not that she hates me or vice versa but we find the excuse of time working in our favour. She believes that I ruined my life by not marrying again. Since I do not agree with her, I prefer avoiding her.'

In those few moments, I realized how strong- mentally and emotionally-Adah was! She knew her mind way too well. Resolute and confident in what she chose, she was different. That made me love her all the more.

'Don't you feel alone at times?' I asked.

'It is strange, isn't it? You know yourself better than anyone else, yet you crumble at the words of someone who hasn't even lived a second of your life. You fail to focus on your voice just because the voices around you are so loud.' Her voice trailed off. She took a moment, paused, stared right into the nothingness and then took a sip of coffee.

'When you put it like that, it sounds right. But when I tell my heart to accept it, it refuses to comply. I still feel that a companion is very important. One cannot survive alone.'

'I don't agree with you. Companionship is like dessert. While we know that food alone can help us survive, we prefer a dessert to complement our meal and make it more delectable. Over time, we forget that survival without dessert is also possible.'

I wondered if Adah's point of view was a result of too much reading or was it a manifestation of her mind.

She continued, 'One day, Avyan, it just clicks! You realize what's important and what isn't. You begin to care less about what people think of you and more about what you think about yourself. You realize how far you have come and think about the time when you almost gave up and thought you would never make through. And you smile. You smile because you are truly proud of yourself and the person you have fought to become.'

'In this process of finding yourself, have you found out the goal of all this detachment from people? Is it worth it?'

'Of course! The goal is to live without any pressure or expectations. The goal is to cherish the memories of the ones I have lost and the ones who love me dearly.'

'What about me then? I am friend-zoned, aren't I?'

'Haha! Not really. I don't understand the intention of using this term in the first place. Just because two people cannot be lovers, it doesn't mean that one of them has been friend-zoned. I doubt if you ever considered me your friend.'

'Come on, I have always considered you my friend.'

'That's not true. You see, Bobby is your friend. You see me as your lover. I learnt to distinguish between relationships only after I lost Darsh. One day, you too will see.'

I glanced at the wall clock. It was 2:30 PM and we had to head back to the office. Having talked for two hours, we still hadn't reached a closure or conclusion. At least, I hadn't.

'Is there no way to think that you might want to give me a chance?' I tried asking.

'I am sorry. I know me. I am not looking for love, leave alone falling in love.'

'What if you change your mind?'

'I won't. You know it too. If you had lost your wife, say for instance, would you ever be able to forget her?'

'I don't know. Maybe, I won't.'

That's true. Losing a loved one and then deciding to move on knowing that memories will fade over time- that thought sent jitters down my spine. I knew what lay ahead and therefore, I decided to give back the reigns of my life to time and fate. Sometimes you continue to suffer if you have an emotional reaction to everything that is said to you. The true power is sitting back and observing things with logic. True power is restraint. I allowed the phase to pass.

We headed back to the office. Adah tried to lighten the mood by talking about the elections and the nominees. I failed to concentrate. She knew that though.

'So, how did it go?' Peter queried.

'Misfire. It was a misfire. They aren't interested.' I replied.

'How can that be? You draft a proposal and I shall look into it. We can get them. Come on, now,' urged Peter.

'It's over, Peter. There is nothing more left to discuss. They don't want to join us. They already have someone in their life, I mean mind,' I heard the irony of my situation echoing in my words.

'He's right, Peter. I got to know from a source that Frisco is not looking for the marketing team at all. There is no point in badgering them.'

Bobby knew or maybe he figured out looking at my glum expressions. He put his hand on Peter's back and guided that fool to his cabin. I wanted to be alone. I wanted to think of every possible argument that I could use to convince Adah.

'It's okay. You will be fine. Come, let's go home.'

'I won't be. Why isn't she willing to give herself a second chance?' I asked Bobby as if he knew all the answers.

'Maybe she doesn't need a second chance. Maybe she is satisfied with what she has. And it will be wrong of you to force a person into believing that they are dissatisfied. Isn't it?'

I did not respond. My mind knew he was right but my heart- such a weak fellow it is!

25

Au Revoir

Hope is like a single white thread. It won't be visible when the light is bright; it is visible when shadows are lurking behind you. It is so weak that a single strong pull can weaken the thread and it might break. I was hanging on by fingernails then. With no respite in sight, I lost the track of time. I ended up being awake until dusk and then fell asleep in the office. That went on for a week. I didn't see Adah at all, hoping that it would soon become a habit and would help me in moving on. Only when Bobby revealed that Adah had not been in the city for a week, I realized that I had to begin the drill all over again once she was back, for avoiding her would be the hardest thing to do.

Adah returned to New York after one week. That one week turned out to be a devastating one for me. I overlooked deadlines and in return, got rebuked by Peter in front of everyone. My eating habits became worse. Eventually, Scarlet had to bear the brunt of my actions. I started looking weak and thin. Peter mocked my diminishing figure saying that it was because my mind was somewhere else rather than being at work. Finally, Bobby decided to spend a weekend with me in my apartment.

'Avy, what's with the mess? You were never so messy,' he commented looking at the stack of dirty clothes on the furniture.

'I haven't had time to clean it all up. Why don't you sit on the bed?' I suggested.

'That's alright. I can help you clean.'

He insisted on that. I had to give in eventually. He was a stubborn chap! We took our own sweet time to place the dirty clothes in the laundry basket, dusting Scarlet's fur from the sofas and wiping the house clean. It took us four hours to make my apartment look spick and span. It looked nice, more welcoming and more comfortable. I knew why Bobby had decided to stay back at my place. He was one of those friends who never left your side, especially when you were vulnerable. We watched a movie thereafter. Scarlet was also happy having someone around. I think she was happier about the fact that her house looked immaculate. I knew she disliked the dirt but only if she could set my mind right!

'Have you thought enough about it?' Bobby asked.

'About what?'

'You know, about Adah.'

'I have been thinking. Honestly, I don't know what to do. I spoke to Nandita about this. She, too, thinks it is best to forego it all. The moment I decide not to think about her, her memories come rushing back to me. Is that how love is?'

'Yes, my friend. Love is like that. It can either build or destroy a person. You haven't even spent enough time with Adah and still, you feel the void in your heart. Imagine what all she would have gone through when she would have lost the love of her life?'

Bobby made complete sense. Suddenly, I felt disgusted with myself. How could I force Adah to leave her husband's memories and fall in love with another man? It was so selfish of me.

'I have wronged her. What do I do now? Should I apologize to her?' I asked.

'You don't need to, my friend. You just need to accept what is before you. That is all that she would like,' Bobby patted my shoulder.

'Will she talk to me again?'

'Why wouldn't she? Did she say anything about not talking to you? No, right? Then don't overthink.'

I slept better that night. One of the major disadvantages of staying away from your family is that you don't have any shoulder to cry on. I thanked Bobby from my heart. I cannot say if I had accepted the reality but one thing was sure that I was ready to attempt. Bobby and I spend another hour lying on the soft mattress, talking about the not-so-important things and eventually fell asleep.

Scarlet's constant tossing and turning woke me up at 5:00 A.M. Yes, she slept with us on the bed. I didn't say anything because my mind was too preoccupied already. With her fur merging well with the beige bed cover, I couldn't help avoid occasional sneezes. That noise woke up Bobby.

'Man, you must get rid of this dog,' whined Bobby.

'You know, she understands what you say,' I warned.

Just then, as if to prove me right, Scarlet pounced on Bobby and barked at him- no, not in anger but in a way that he understood what he had said was wrong!

It was Sunday and we decided to head out for a nice run and then grab something to eat while returning. That was not the first time I was going for a run. I might not be a fitness enthusiast but I liked indulging in a cardio activity once in a while.

'So, how are things at your end?' I asked Bobby, attempting at the small talk.

'Come on, you know how they are. I am still looking for a better opportunity. What about you? Are you still keen on working here in NYT?'

'Not really. I want to avoid Adah without making it too obvious for her and I also want to get rid of Peter. I know he wouldn't give any chance to my career to soar! Such a selfish brute he is!'

'That is true. I heard about an opening for a Marketing Manager in Brooklyn Eagle. Are you interested?'

'Wouldn't that be a demotion?' I asked.

'Not really. It is one of the oldest newspapers. It might not have that kind of following but I have heard that people are nice there. Also, you will move away from here.'

'That seems fitting. How far is Brooklyn? 7 miles?'

'Yes, approximately.'

That seemed like a feasible option. I thought of confronting Adah first and then applying for the position.

The next day, Bobby and I reached the office a little early. I had a pending proposal to proofread and Bobby had promised to help me with that.

While I was rummaging through my drawer to find the paperclip, a sudden tap on the table grabbed my attention. I looked up to find Adah standing there.

'Hi, how come you are here?' I asked.

'I was out of the city for some work. I returned a few days back so I thought of catching up with you. How have you been?'

'Don't worry. I gave it all a lot of thought. I am better now. It took me some time to understand your point of view and now, trust me, I am coping well.'

'I am glad to hear that. Would like to have lunch then? Where is Bobby? Let's all catch up,' she offered.

'Are you sure?' I confirmed.

'Yes. Tanny will be coming over to meet me so I thought of inviting you both as well. She is leaving for Canada tomorrow. She has got a new job. So, this might as well be her farewell lunch.'

'Oh, that's bad. I am going to miss her,' chirped Bobby.

'Oh really, Bob? How close were you two by the way?' I asked.

He just gestured to me to shut up. He knew how to ease the tension out. He could always do that.

I met Adah at Capizzi for lunch. The four of us had a good time. We didn't talk about 'us'. We talked about everything else. At one point, Bobby was about to blurt out that I might take up the new job at Brooklyn Eagle. But I stopped him. I didn't want Adah to feel that I was changing the job because of her. I knew she would be upset and end up doing something that she didn't want to do. I didn't want that.

We finished lunch and headed back to work. Somewhere Cole's farewell seemed like a farewell to my love life as well.

I had that feeling that I was ready to move on. I went back home and applied for the job that Bobby had told me about. It was after a month that I got a response from them. They had scheduled an interview for me. I cracked it. And soon I moved to Brooklyn. By that time, Adah and I had maintained a mutual distance. We talked only when it was necessary or when we had our friends around us. That was my unsaid rule. She just played along. I had a faint hope that she would come up to me one day and ask me to patch up things, for she would also be in love with me. But that only happens in movies, isn't it? In real life, the bed of roses often has a lot of thorns. Scarlet was sad too. She liked her home in New York. The one in Brooklyn was too big for the two of us. She loved the space as much as she hated the light.

Life was getting back to normal. Often when I would visit Bobby, who was still working in NYT, I would spot Adah in the office premises. We would exchange genial greetings and nothing more.

'How is she doing?' I would often ask Bobby.

'She is doing well. We talk once in a while. She misses your company but she misses Cole too. So, there is no point in getting excited.' Bobby would answer.

And then one day, I told Bobby that I was over her. It had been seven months since I had moved to Brooklyn. And I had come to grips with the fact that Adah wouldn't be a part of my life.

Epilogue

3 Years Later

The bustling city of Delhi had no respite for aching ears. There was noise all around- cars honking, tyres screeching, temple bells ringing incessantly and dogs barking. All this didn't happen simultaneously. It happened one after the other. I was there for one week. My parents' constant badgering had finally forced me to book tickets and visit home. It was a homecoming after a long time! The streets seemed familiar though a lot had changed. New people could be seen in our society. The old ones were still there. Umpteen number of children could be seen running about shouting their lungs off!

'Come in, come in. Oh, we have waited for this moment for such a long time,' greeted my mother, 'how have you been?' She forced a close hug. I felt a little uncomfortable. I had lost the sense of human touch. Back there in New York, I had become used to being along. A casual brushing of shoulders or a peck on the cheek was all that my body accepted now. The full-fledged hug felt uncanny and I cringed.

'Look at you! Still the same, aren't you?' My aunty commented.

'Aunty Lobo, what a pleasant surprise! When did you come from Jaipur?' I couldn't help asking.

'I came just yesterday. Your father pestered me to come and meet you. And then I thought why not have the conversation with you face-to-face!'

'Which conversation?' My mind dreaded the response, for I already knew the answer.

'Come on, let's sit and have tea. It's too cold to be out here chatting,' intruded my father.

The winnowing wind brushed the parted strands of my hair as if trying to cheer my up. I sat in the verandah, sipping hot tomato soup that my mother had prepared. It was cold. I could imagine my fingers turn blue if the glove was not in place. It felt nice and warm being home after a long time. Though none of my family members had spoken about re-marriage again, I just hoped they didn't. Aadrika was not home. She had gone to Himachal with her friends. And that provided me with the much-needed solitude. After Avyan shifted to Brooklyn, I didn't have any common or logical reason to chat with Bobby either. In a way, I lost my two friends even before our friendship could brew. Tanny had already moved to Canada. Knowing that it would be hard for me to reach out and make new friends, I decided to get a dog because I remembered how Avyan always praised Scarlet and appreciated his decision of taking her in. I named my dog Lorry. Over a period of two months, Lorry and I became quite close. He kept me company and I liked his presence. Being here in Delhi made me remember him and miss him daily. I had left him in a dog shelter for 15 days that I was supposed to spend with my parents. Alas! I missed him.

Later that day, my father urged me to get dressed as he had planned a dinner. Before agreeing to his invitation, I asked him if he had invited any other family members. He denied.

'Order whatever you like,' he smiled.

'Really? What's gone into you? Why are you being so nice?' I smirked.

'It's just that we have missed you a lot. In your absence, we realized that if we had not forced our decisions upon you, you would have not gone so far,' he admitted.

I think I saw a tear escape the corner of his eye. There was an uncomfortable silence at the table. I expected my mother to speak as well. But she didn't.

'Papa, you need not say all this. Now that I am here, let's enjoy the food and our time together. So, what do you want to do tonight? UNO, Monopoly or Rummy?' I tried to cheer him up.

'Tonight? Nothing tonight,' said my mother.

'Why not?' I asked.

'Lobo aunty wants to come over and talk to you,' she replied.

'About what? Can't she wait till tomorrow? I have just come back home and I am going to stay for another two weeks. What's the hurry?'

'She just wants to get over with it. You know, it will take time to convince y...'

'Can you not talk about all this?' interrupted my father.

'You know that Lobo has been planning this for a long time.'

'Yes, I know and now I regret that I didn't stop her.' My father said remorsefully.

'Will someone tell me what is this all about?' I asked.

'Your aunt Lobo and your mother are trying to find a match for you. I know this upsets you. But I cannot hold this within me any longer. Why can't we just leave Adah alone? Why do you still want to interfere in her life?' He asked my mother as if on the verge of breaking down.

We didn't talk about it later that day. Aunt Lobo wasn't allowed in the house for another week. My father called her up and made an excuse saying that I had gone out with my friends. Aunt Lobo wasn't an easy cookie to crack. Thus, she asked if I had any friends left in Delhi. At that, my father took Vidhi's name and urged me to find out if Vidhi was free and if I could plan something with her.

'But I came back to spend time with you,' I protested.

'The longer you stay here, the more people will barge into your privacy. I do not want to let you go on bad terms this time. I want to make things right. Spend time with your friends and we will spend enough time together next week.'

Listening to my father's words made me realize how far I had come. I missed those times when all was well when I was still in school and my mother and my father cared more about me than the society. I missed the time when I could share my apprehensions with my family, well, at least some of them. Now, I had become used to keeping my fears and joys to myself. I liked it that way. As a result, I couldn't even tell my father how much I appreciated his gesture.

Well, that's how I ended up in Munnar after the conversation at dinner. Vidhi and I planned to spend five days exploring the hill station. I always liked the mountains. Travelling too! And travelling with Vidhi felt like a long due relaxation period. We spent the first day exploring different market areas and viewpoints and spent the first-night chatting and catching up on each other's life. It was on the second last day of our trip that I saw Avyan in the lobby of our hotel. Hesitant at first, I made the first move and called out to him.

'Hi,' he clearly looked shocked.

'How come you are here?' I asked.

'Well, I came on a vacation,' he answered. The lump in his throat was quite evident. He was reluctant to share the details and that made me more curious.

'Vacation? Alone?'

'Umm...with my wife,' he clarified.

Just then he turned around and called out to Raveena, his wife. She was pretty. Her skin looked as fresh as the first snow. She looked so much in love. Suddenly, I realized why Avyan had been hesitant about sharing that information. But then I thought about us. We never had a thing. Or maybe it was difficult for him to admit before me that he had moved on. What did I expect him to do? I didn't know. I hadn't thought about it.

'That's wonderful news. Congratulations to you two!' I said.

'Why don't you join us for lunch?' Raveena invited me with genuine sincerity.

'I am sure Adah is busy. She is always busy,' interrupted Avyan.

I didn't quite like his rude remark. He wasn't like that. Maybe he changed with time. It had been three years already.

'When did you get married? Even Bobby didn't tell me,' I said.

'A year and a half back. Bobby has been busy with his life, I guess,' he responded.

Just then Avyan turned towards Raveena and gestured something. She smiled and said, 'He is playing in the garden.'

Seeing my confused look, Raveena told me about their son who was outside. Caught unawares, I looked at Avyan in amazement. He had a kid! I couldn't have thought of it in my wildest imagination. Still, I knew that I was happy for him. Partly because his marriage and his fatherhood meant that he no longer accused me of ruining his life. He never actually accused me of anything. It's something that I thought he would do.

'What's his name?' I inquired.

'Arya,' he answered.

'Such a beautiful name. I hope we meet sometime soon in New York.'

'I don't live there anymore. I moved back to Mumbai after completing a year at Brooklyn Eagle. That's when my parents and Raveena's parents fixed our alliance. Shortly after that initial dating, we decided to tie the knot. That's my story.' He said.

'That's good to hear.' Just then Raveena excused herself to go and check up on Arya. Avyan seemed more comfortable than before.

'What's up with you? How come you are here?'

'I came with one of my friends, Vidhi, for a short trip. We are leaving for Delhi tomorrow.'

'Have you too shifted to Delhi?' He sounded a little happy.

'That's not going to happen. I am still there at NYT. I do have Lorry for company now. He is adorable.'

'And Lorry is…'

'My dog,' I said before Avyan could jump to any conclusions.

'Aren't you planning on coming back?'

Suddenly I remembered my father's words and his worried face. It would mean the world to him if I decided to return home. But that would snatch away my peace of mind. And thus, I brushed aside the thought.

'No. I am happy and content there. That's my home now.'

I saw an ambiguous emotion engulf Avyan. From what I could gather, I knew he wanted to be sad about it but then there was a frightening glint in his eyes.

Are you happy about this? About me not coming back? I wanted to ask but I didn't.

'I am happy because I do not want to walk the same road again. If you are here before me, I know I will falter and unintentionally compromise my future with my family.' He clarified as if he had already read my mind.

'What if I say that I am ready to give you a second chance now?' I spoke trying to test the waters.

'I think I get it. You didn't want a second chance before. I do not want one now. If I take this second chance, I would have to lose my loved ones and break many hearts. Even though our circumstances are different, I now understand why you did what you did.'

I breathed a sigh of relief. There was the closure I sought. I smiled and so did he. We didn't speak after that. Words weren't required. It felt like a heavy load had been lifted and my shoulders felt light again. We parted ways with a slight hug.

Upon reaching Delhi, I saw the glint in my father's eyes as he stood by the door. His frame had shrunken over the years. He was old. My mother, too, was frail. But she was still the same stubborn woman. One night, I asked my father if he wanted me to stay and he politely refused. He knew that I would become obliged to stay back and he also knew that by doing that he would make me kiss happiness goodbye. He understood. I was happy that after so many years, at least someone understood. I bid goodbye to my family the next week and headed to where I felt home. My old friends, the genial humans of the Senior Citizen Carehouse, waited for me eagerly. I had missed visiting them for two weeks and I already felt a void in my heart. It was because of Avyan that I started mingling with people more often, for he always advised me to become more friendly. Since I couldn't adjust well with new people, I decided to contribute to the Senior Citizens Carehouse. And I began liking it. My life in New York was comfortable. I did not have many visitors but I found solace in the work that I did. In three years, I had garnered enough praise for my work and that was what kept me going. As far as Darsh was concerned, he had never left my heart.

ACKNOWLEDGEMENTS

If I were to dedicate this page to one person, it would be my dearest husband without whom you wouldn't be holding this dream of mine in your hands. His unceasing support and critical evaluations led to the completion of this book in its best form. While I was stuck between what I wanted and what my readers suggested, my husband showed me the way and encouraged me to follow my heart. Thank you and I love you, Harsh!

Thank you, mom, for making me a strong woman and my brother, Shantanu, for being my best supporter. Even if I don't say it enough, I want you to know that I love you both more than the stars love the sky. My in-laws played a very important role in the conception of this book as well. Their cheers and encouragement kept me going! I am grateful to my friends who stood by me during the thick and the thin and provided their valuable feedback even when I asked for suggestions at odd hours. You all are my pillars of strength and I could not have done this without you.

My words aren't enough to thank Abhisar from Inkquills Publishing House who was kind enough to deal with my bizarre queries and provide help whenever asked. He is such a wonderful person to work with.

I thank my brilliant brain for bearing with my irregular writing schedule. It was patient enough to hold the threads of the story together for long. Also, kudos to Gibbs, my dog, who didn't jump on my laptop when I spent my time typing rather than cuddling with him!

Last but not the least, I am thankful to my readers. None of this would have been possible without you. I never lose sight of that and I never will. I love you all to the moon and back.

Before you close the book:

Remember to let your soul breathe freedom.

Let it enjoy what it likes.

Make others a part of your life.

Give life a second chance.

Let love in.

Choice yourself and be happy.

Enakshi J.

Enakshi J. is an educator, author and traveller. Her articles have appeared in *The Speaking Tree (Times of India)*, *Woman's Era*, *Alive*, *Infinithoughts*, *SivanaSpirit*, *Women's Web*, *EfictionIndia* and *Induswomanwriting*. Her stories and poems have been anthologized widely. She writes a weekly editorial, *Odds and Evens*, for a Social Journalism platform called *Different Truths*. She has conceptualized and edited three books- *Unbounded Trajectories*, *Poison Ivy* and *Cryptic Encounters*. Her poetry collection, *The Green Giants*, released this year.

Find her at aliveshadow.com.

Instagram: @enakshijohri12

Facebook: @enakshi.johri12

THE GREEN GIANTS
And Other Poems
Enakshi J